LONGHAND

BY THE SAME AUTHOR

The Star Witness

ANDY HAMILTON

LONGHAND

First published in 2020

Unbound
T C Group, Level 1 Devonshire House, One Mayfair Place, London W1J 8AJ
www.unbound.com

A CIP record for this book is available from the British Library

ISBN 978-1-78352-941-4 (hardback edition)
ISBN 978-1-78352-942-1 (ebook)

Printed in Great Britain by CPI Group (UK)

1 3 5 7 9 8 6 4 2

With special thanks
Caroline Orr
Gabriella 'Nonna' Penfold

Ifield, Timothy and McCreadle
Solicitors
14 High Street
Forres
IV36 1DB

To: **John Mitchinson**
Unbound
48 Wharf Road
London N1 7UX

Date: **11th February 2020**
Your ref:
Our ref: **NKM:1DAL20**

Dear John,

Further to our conversation, please find enclosed the hand-written manuscript that I discussed with you. As you can see, it takes the form of a substantial letter that our client, Ms Elizabeth Dalglish, discovered hidden in her house.

The missive was left for her by My Malcolm Galbraith, her partner. It appears to have been written over a couple of days and provides, in part at least, the unverifiable account of why he disappeared so suddenly.

You may recall that he went missing in dramatic and mysterious circumstances that attracted considerable media speculation, not just up here in Scotland but across the entire UK and indeed beyond.

To that end, she is prepared to release the letter into the public domain in the hope that the attendant publicity might prompt Mr Galbraith to make contact, or at least increase the chances of someone reporting his whereabouts.

It is clear from the letter that Mr Galbraith is in a distressed state of mind and needs help and support. Needless to say, our client cannot vouch for the veracity of any of the contents of any of the claims made by Mr Galbraith. readers will have to reach their own conclusions.

Should you choose to publish, our client is prepared to waive any financial stake in the interests of locating Mr Galbraith.

I look forward to hearing from you.

Yours sincerely,

Neville McCreadle

1

29th November
00.15 a.m.

My darling Bess,

What the hell is this? That's what you're thinking right now. I will have hidden this letter in a place where I know only you could find it (I haven't worked out where that is yet) and, now that you've found it, you are probably turning the air blue because nobody swears as imaginatively or as beautifully as you, Bessie.

Well, that's a totally proper and understandable reaction in the light of such distressing circumstances.

I am so sorry that I have abandoned you in this terrible way, but staying would have placed you in grave danger.

What you're about to read is a love-letter. I'll try to avoid soppiness. I know you hate that. It's also a story – my story. Some parts of my story are shocking, some are comic; some are both.

There are murders, battles, betrayal, vengeance, corruption, lions and, eventually, love.

You're the final chapter.

You are the first person to hear this story. I've never felt safe enough with anyone else to entrust them with it.

You're unique.

I'm writing in longhand for the simple reason that I smashed up my laptop.

I pounded it into wee tiny bits and then threw the pieces into the river.

I'd had a bad day.

I'm sorry I told you that it had been stolen. Just one of many necessary lies, I'm afraid.

But, as it turns out, I'm glad to be writing it this way. It feels more personal, and certainly more private because <u>nothing</u> is private on a computer these days.

As you read on, there will be moments when you'll probably presume that I've gone insane.

But I promise you that I'm not insane.

I have *been* insane, several times. But never during our twenty years together and definitely not now.

My plan is to write this in the night while you are sleeping. At this moment, I'm up in the loft, cocooned in several layers of clothing because it is so bloody cold. (I think the boiler's on the blink again. I'll look at it, if I get time)

This has to be written as fast as possible and under considerable emotional pressure, so you may have to put up with a few crossings-out.

I know that you teachers like everything to be tidy, but I won't have time for perfectionism.

Also, Bessie, the style and the tone will not be up to your high standards, due to the fact that I am in one hell of a state.

He has got me seriously

rattled. Deep down, I suppose I knew this day would come, but my time with you made me hope that He had forgotten me.

But one thing I can promise you is that everything I write will be 100% accurate. Every detail will be correct because I am blessed, and cursed, with a photographic memory.

I never forget a single look or word, no matter how hard I try.

On the upside, we have won a lot of pub quizzes, haven't we. I will miss those. And many other things besides.

We've had a wonderful twenty years, Bessie. The best twenty years of my life, in fact. Ultimately, I think, every human being is alone, but sharing our loneliness and transforming it into some indefinable intimacy has been a magical experience. (Sorry. I know. Soppy)

Sadly, however, things are

not as they appear.

For two decades, you've been living with Malcolm Galbraith — an implausibly huge man with a very soft Scottish accent that some people find difficult to place.

That's another thing that I'm going to miss. I've enjoyed having a mild Scottish accent. Not all accents are as gentle on the ear.

According to my passport (forged), my full name is Malcolm George Galbraith and I have been proud to be Malcolm George Galbraith because people like him and feel they can rely on him.

Malcolm is someone who never changes. He looks the same now as he did twenty years ago. He's a constant in a changing, turbulent world. No wonder people warm to him. He's a good man.

Well, he is an alias. Another of my necessary lies, I'm afraid

I've no idea how much time I'll get to set this down, so I'd better dive in and reveal who I really am.

My name is Heracles and I think I may be immortal.

It looks ridiculous written down, I've never done that before.

I 'think' I may be immortal because, thus far, I have found it impossible to die.

Despite my best efforts – countless efforts, spanning thousands of years – I've not been able to destroy myself.

My last attempt, in 1991, ended farcically when I leapt off a motorway bridge and landed on a farm vehicle, killing several sheep. (It ended up in all the newspapers. Alan Coren made jokes about it on Radio Four – very funny ones, I couldn't help but laugh)

I'm guessing, my love, that you're telling yourself that your poor Malcolm has clearly had some kind of mental breakdown and needs medical help.

But admit it, Bessie, deep down, you've always sensed that I'm not what I appear to be. Often I've caught you watching me with that questioning spark in your eye.

Malcolm is just the latest in a long list of identities that I've adopted through many, many centuries.

In fact, I've lost track now of exactly how old I am. It's quite complicated because so many of those early civilizations kept messing around with their calendars.

Let's just say that I am five thousand-ish and almost certainly the oldest living thing on this planet — with the possible exception of a tree in Perthshire.

It's a yew. It stands in the churchyard of a village called Fortingall. In times of crisis, I've often sat and stared at this tree in silent kinship.

I mustn't get sidetracked by trees, there's a lot to get through.

Right this second, I'm trying to picture your beautiful face as you struggle to take all this in.

I had no choice but to disappear, Bessie. You'd have got caught in the crossfire. He doesn't care about collateral damage. To Him, people are just toys.

Clearly, the fact that I've lied to you for twenty years is bound to raise some trust issues.

Understatement. I learnt that from you.

But what would it have achieved if I'd dropped this truth-bomb at the start of our relationship?

You'd have dumped me for sure.

You'd have probably taken out a restraining order against the massive weirdo who claims he's depicted on vases.

There were hundreds of occasions when I wanted to tell you everything, but I was always too scared.

What if I'd lost you?

For twenty years, I've been warmed by your smile and thrilled by the sound of your key in the door.

If I hadn't lied, I'd have missed out on all of that. (I know. Not an excuse)

The story I'm aiming to tell is certain to get a wee bit chaotic because, from the day I was born, chaos has been my constant companion.

I've bottled all this up for so long that, once I start, I expect it'll pour out of me. I've no idea how much I'll end up writing. But I've got a lot of pens!

To keep things simple, I'll begin at the very beginning. In Ancient Thebes – or, as it was known then, Thebes.

My birth-name was Alceides. That's one of the very few details of my story that the mythographers actually got right.

At an early age, for absurd reasons, I was re-named Heracles. According to the legend, I am currently in Heaven, having been poisoned by a vengeful centaur and a jealous wife.

The agony that they inflicted on me was supposedly ended when Zeus took pity on my plight (yeh, 'course he did) and took me up to Mount Olympus where I could enjoy a peaceful, eternal retirement.

And yet here I am, sitting in a cold loft, as I look out over the still, moonlit waters of the Moray Firth. Here, I'm an odd-job man and gardener. Not the kind of feats that'll ever inspire a statue or mosaic.

In the myth, my father's name is Amphitryon which, surprisingly, also turns out to be correct. He was my father in the sense that he raised me and loved me and got nothing in return, apart from some broken ribs and a betrayal. (I was not a good son, Bessie. I was a brat)

My biological father, of course, again, according to the legend, was Zeus, King of the Gods.

That could well be true. But, there again, Zeus is also King of The Liars.

Not for the first time tonight, I can hear the pop-pop-pop of fireworks. That'll be the MacKenzie boys terrorising the estate.

They're not the brightest, are they. (Yes, I know, two of them have been diagnosed with syndromes.)

What is it with mankind and loud bangs?

Several thousand years ago I watched some excited Chinese engineers explaining to a local warlord that they were about to demonstrate their latest invention — the combustible dust that we know as gunpowder.

A few moments later, limbs were hanging from the trees like fruit.

But the love-affair had begun.

Back to the King of the Liars. Zeus has been the bane of my existence and yet, according to the myth, it's not He who has persecuted me but his wife, Hera, who hated me from day one.

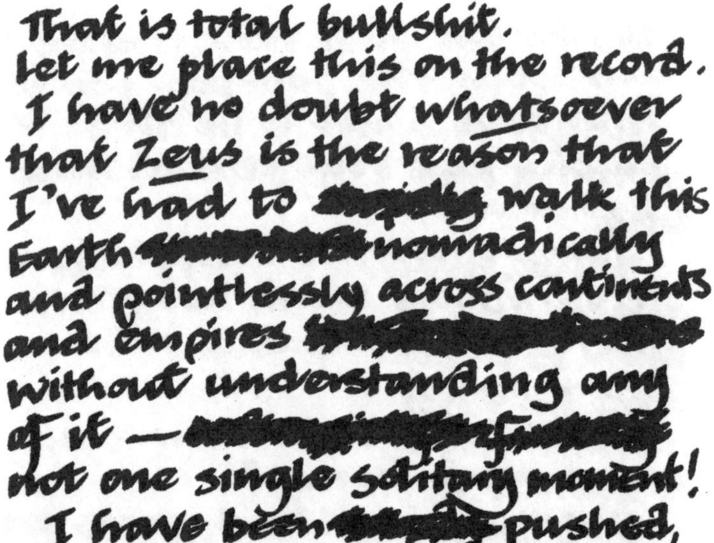

That is total bullshit.
Let me place this on the record.
I have no doubt whatsoever that Zeus is the reason that I've had to walk this Earth nomadically and pointlessly across continents and empires without understanding any of it — not one single solitary moment!

I have been pushed, pulled, dragged and jerked around like someone's leashed puppy!!!

I think I'd better stop for a bit.

Maybe go for a run. Clear my head.

It's important that I don't let my temper get the better of me.

That's how I ended up killing my music teacher.

13

Alright, it's just gone two in the morning and I've calmed down now.

You're probably a little taken aback. The Malcolm that you know is a composed, patient man. And he's not a lie. One of the advantages of living for thousands of years is that you do learn the art of patience – you have no choice.

So, yes, I have become pretty adept at managing my emotions, but there are still times when I need to let off steam.

Of course, what 'normal' men do in that situation is go out and get drunk. But that option's not available to me, because alcohol turns me into someone else.

I ran to Culbin Forest. I sprinted deep into the comforting darkness of the woods and I checked and double-checked that there was no-one else around.

I called out, just in case

there were people hidden from view. I made totally, absolutely sure that I was alone.

And then I vented my rage, responsibly. I won't go into details, let's just say a few trees got pushed over.

An abandoned car also took a bit of a pounding. (At least, I *hope* it was abandoned)

When you possess freakish and prodigious strength, you have to be careful not to alarm people. I've never let you witness any extraordinary feats – with the possible exception of the time when I hauled that cow out of the river. You asked a lot of questions about how on earth I'd managed it, do you remember? I fobbed you off with some nonsense about the power of adrenaline, but I could tell that I'd spooked you.

When I was a young man, I used to love demonstrating how astonishingly strong I was. Sometimes I'd push a building over, just to show off.

But, nowadays, I don't want any attention at all.

Ok, let's go back to my beginnings. I need to crack on because although *I* may have all the time in the world, the clock is ticking for *us*.

I know this to be true because of the things you told me at breakfast ~~this morning~~ yesterday morning. You dropped a real bombshell without realizing it, my love.

But I'm getting ahead of myself. Let's get back to the Divine Ratbag. As I said, I am very confident that the goddess Hera's infamous animosity towards me is/was non-existent.

How can I be sure? Well I've no absolute proof, but I'd wager any money that Hera herself does not exist. I base this on the following observations.

One: Though I've encountered Zeus, in person, on many occasions, I have never – at least, not to my knowledge – met Hera.

Two: In all my interactions with Zeus, he's never mentioned Hera. He's certainly never mentioned a wife. Nor has he mentioned Apollo, Poseidon, Athena or any of that menagerie of emotional defectives that the Greeks chose to worship.

My guess is that Zeus is the only God, but that the Greeks devised additional deities to try and make sense of all his many personalities. Because he is utterly bewildering.

One moment he's moral, the next he's a rapist. He is so erratic and capricious, his actions are so unfathomable and chaotic that, as a character, he just doesn't hang together.

He's a mess of contradictions.

I told him that once.

It didn't go down well.

Of course, the other reason why the Greeks opted for a pantheon was probably money.

Many gods meant many temples and many shrines. Many cults meant many meal-tickets for all the oracles, priests, charm-sellers, food-vendors, prostitutes, mystics and general pilgrim-fleecers.

For most of the time, the various cults managed to co-exist. But if one became too dominant, that was when the swords came out.

When I was born, in Thebes, the pantheon of gods were an unquestioned reality. (I know, Bessie, bad grammar, apologies) Everyone believed in them, and in a whole supporting cast of fantastical, supernatural creatures.

I believed, 100%, in the existence of beings that were half-man and half-horse, or half-man and half-bull, or half-man and half-chicken. (That legend didn't stand the test of time for some reason)

We all believed, intensely, that the world was being carried on the shoulders of a giant and that you could make deals with the gods of Death.

Were we more stupid and credulous back then? Perhaps we were.

But there again, last Tuesday Mrs. Mac refused to go anywhere near the kettle because the Daily Express astrologer had warned her that she might experience problems with an electrical appliance.

People have always believed in things that are rampant bullshit. It's a basic human need.

Very, *very* occasionally the nonsense may stem from some tiny grain of truth.

For example, take the legend of the wily Oddyseus. (Yes, that is how I'm spelling it. I don't care what your Encyclopaedia says and no, I'm not having a bet)

I can confirm that there was such a man as Oddyseus and he did fight at Troy.

I met him in Ithaca some years after the war had ended. To him, I was a shepherd named Paxo (like the man you heckle during University Challenge)

By that time, the tall stories about Oddyseus had mushroomed to such an extent that he was finding them intolerable.

Once, I saw him encircled by

wide-eyed youths who begged him to tell the story of how he'd vanquished the mighty Cyclops.

Rolling his eyes, Oddyseus explained that, shortly after the fall of Troy, he'd commissioned a local blacksmith to re-shoe the horses of his platoon.

The Greek army had its own blacksmith, but he was notorious for his shoddy workmanship. The Trojan, on the other hand, was skilled and quoted a reasonable price—3 sheep.

However, when Oddyseus came to pay him, the blacksmith complained that the sheep were too small. Oddyseus replied that the sheep were sheep-sized, but now the blacksmith said that, if miniature sheep were the currency, then he wanted six.

Oddyseus didn't want a confrontation. After the destruction of Troy, the Greek soldiers had been ordered to try and win hearts and minds. (They failed.)

The blacksmith was offered a fourth sheep, but he became aggressive and began to advance on the Greek, who was unaccompanied and unarmed.

As the blacksmith – who was big even by blacksmith standards – shaped to punch him, Oddyseus plucked a poker from the fire and shoved the red-hot end into the blacksmith's eye. The 'giant' fell, screaming to the floor. Oddyseus left with the sheep.

The incident caused a few ripples. Some locals complained to King Agamemnon that one of their citizens had been half-blinded by one of ~~their~~ his men. But, as Oddyseus had never given his name and there were no witnesses, the matter went no further.

That, Oddyseus explained to those star-struck lads, was the distant ancestor of the Cyclops story. It had a big man who became one-eyed, a question-mark over the name of his assailant, and it involved some sheep.

Beyond that, it bore no resemblance to the tale that so excited them.

Well, he'd been wasting his breath. His young fans accused him of inventing this version out of a sense of modesty. They saluted his humility, but continued to believe the story that they wanted to believe.

In the end, Oddyseus gave up trying to set the record straight.

The originator of the fantastical stories was one of his crew members, Thyrates, who made a fortune sitting outside theatres with his hat on the ground, as he acted out his yarns to the crowd.

After a few years, he had separated so many coins from so many idiots that he was able to buy an enormous mansion, complete with flamingoes.

And, instead of telling the stories himself, he ended up employing young bards to tour the Aegean declaiming the epic adventures of Oddyseus.

This franchise thrived many years before Homer happened along.

Oddyseus hated all of it.

Most of all, he hated how the legend devalued the achievement that gave him the most pride.

He'd survived the Trojan war, which was more than most, and even more impressively he'd survived the long, perilous sea-journey home; riding out storms, shipwrecks and black periods of depression.

He'd talk to me about all this, while we sat in the hills, escaping from society.

But remarkably, despite all the dangers, he had *not* lost one, single crew-member. A hell of a feat.

Yet according to the legend he lost dozens of men – most of them devoured. It enraged him that he wouldn't be remembered for the near-miracle of getting *all* his men safely home (including that weasel Thyrates).

I think he wouldn't have got so low if Penelope had stayed.

By the time he'd returned from the war, they were both changed people. For a while, they stayed together in a comfortable friendship, quietly mourning the spark.

Then, one day, she told him that she'd met someone and she wanted to be released from her vows.

So, Oddyseus let her go. Another example of his personal heroism that did not find its way into the legend.

The last time I saw him he was waving from the headland, as I sailed out of the harbour.'

A few years later, I heard that he'd been found hanging from the tree that grew through the middle of his house.

Oddyseus hated his legend because he felt that all the fictions diminished him.

I feel the same way about mine. I hadn't intended to write so much about Oddyseus, but I often find myself thinking about him.

Sorry, Bessie, it's all turned a bit sad and you're always telling me that you've got no time for 'sad'.

On the subject of absurd fictions, and in the interests of speed, I'm going to whizz through the myth of Heracles and dispose of all the inaccuracies and rampant bullshittery.

It's already gone four and you usually get up at six, so I need to crack on. So let's dispense with them, in no particular order.

1. I was given to Hera as a baby. But when she fed me I bit so hard that milk squirted from her breast and formed the Milky Way.

Surprisingly, this turns out to be garbage.

2. I had a twin brother called Iphicles.

No. My brother (not really a twin) was called Xantes. I never met anyone called Iphicles.

3. As a baby, I strangled 2 snakes.

Possibly.

This is a story that my parents loved to tell, though the snakes did grow in size as the years went by.

I was a very strong and very big baby. My hands, apparently, were extremely powerful and strikingly long.

In fact, my infant nickname was 'Zeal' – which, in Theban

dialect, meant 'Longhands'.
So I'd probably have been capable of strangling snakes – however the hell you do that.

And there were lots of snakes in the hills – wee yellow and black stripey ones, mildly venomous.

Babies smell of milk, so I suppose the occasional asp might have slithered into a cot.

My mother – who loved complaining – was forever writing to the authorities about the snake-problem.

From time to time, Thebans took to the hills and battered all the snakes they could find with big sticks.
But it never seemed to make much difference.

4. My brother died alongside me in battle.

No. It was far less heroic. He was 19 years old and, sadly, he fell in with a crowd of 'thinkers'.

One night, after many drinks, these philosophers began discussing Geometry and my brother was killed in an argument over a triangle.

I know that must sound ridiculous to you, but in all societies young men get drunk and find things to fight about and, in those days, one of them was Geometry.

Are triangles any more absurd than Celtic versus Rangers?

5. I fathered 50 sons in one night with the daughters of King Thespius.

No. I think I'd remember that. I've no idea who King Thespius was.

6. I saved Thebes from the army of King Erginus.

Well, sort of. I'm not sure you can classify it as an army.

7 I cleaned the stables of King Augeias in one day

Let's get this straight. I did not manage that in one day.

Those stables were in an absolutely unbelievable state, ramshackle, neglected, totally unsanitary.

Many of the animals (it wasn't just horses) were suffering from a disease that made them flail and stagger around like lunatics.

The ground was carpeted with dead creatures. Heaps of dried dung blocked every path. For miles around, nothing grew. No birds flew overhead. When you tried to work, you choked on the flies and the stench.

In all my years on this planet, I've never seen anything like it. And yet, within twenty months, and using a small team of labourers, I'd removed all the towering walls of excrement and rebuilt the stables to a standard that was acknowledged as the epitome of modern design.

At *no* point, did I do anything as crude, or as environmentally harmful, as re-directing a river. What I achieved was *not* the result of some circus strong-man doing a party trick!

I created a network of drainage and irrigation that Brunel would have been proud of. And it would have been admired down through the centuries, if it hadn't been for the earthquake.

No prizes for guessing who was behind that.

8. I killed the mighty Nemean lion.

I killed a lion. But not in Nemea.

9. I killed the seven-headed Hydra.

Never killed a Hydra, never seen one, never met anyone who's seen one. (Apart from a mushroom-munching priest in Corinth who was clearly off his face)

10. I captured the Bear of Erymanthus.

Total bullshit.

11. I captured the Hind of Cerynaica

See 10.

12. I captured the Cretan Bull

No.

13. I rounded up the man-eating mares of King Diomedes, trained them, and then fed him to them.

No, no and no.

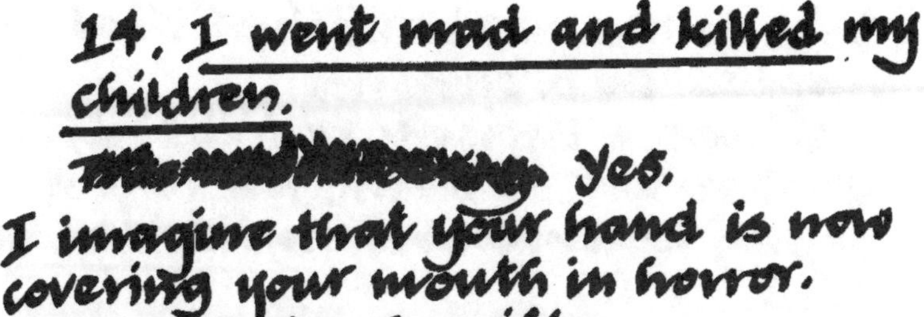

14. I went mad and killed my children.

Yes.

I imagine that your hand is now covering your mouth in horror. Well, it's horrific.

The facts are inescapable — although I did *not* kill my wife. *Some* versions of the legend accuse me of that and they are *wrong*.

What can I say? Your Malcolm? A child-killer?

Perhaps you're telling yourself that these are the imaginings of a madman.

But who could be mad enough to imagine something like that?

I'll write about them when I can find the courage, Bessie.

When I get to their place in the story. If I get there.

So why now? Why, after all this time, am I inflicting these toxic, terrible secrets on you?

It's because time is short, Bessie and I need you to know everything. He is on the prowl; which takes us back to the wee bombshell that you dropped at breakfast.

It was a typical, relaxed, slow start to our Sunday. You're probably trying to remember the things you said.

You were telling me about the new history project you'd started with your third years. You were surprised by how much I knew about the Etruscans.

Then you were interrupted by a phone call from your brother. Ross was a player short for his footie team and did I fancy a game?.

I declined, as I always have before, whenever he's asked.

But you told Ross we'd call him back. And then you did a bit of a number on me.

You switched your beautiful eyes on to full beam and said that Ross had sounded desparate and that he was having a really rough time at the moment and that it would be really nice if I could help him out.

Foolishly, very foolishly, because I wanted to please you, my love,

I agreed to play, even though I had not played any team sport since the late 1800s. (A rugby match that was abandoned after twenty minutes because I'd unintentionally reduced the opposition to eight players)

I should have said no. But, if I stipulated that I had to play in goal, I figured that I could probably avoid causing any damage. (Wrong again, Malcolm!)

You said you'd come and watch the game, once you'd finished your report on Billy Ballantyne's latest suspension.

To be honest, Bessie, you'd spoken so often about this boy that when you started telling me about how he'd gone berserk in assembly, I found myself tuning you out. (Sorry, my love, but this happens in all couples, doesn't it? Even happy ones).

I'd often heard how you felt sorry for Billy because he had no Mum and his father was – I quote – 'a big, fat, mouthy bastard'. You felt that Billy was crippled with insecurity which meant that he didn't connect with the other kids,

except with his fists
By this stage, I'd almost zoned out.
But then you said that the latest,
more worrying development was
that Billy had started complaining
of hallucinations.
I asked what kind of hallucinations.
"A white stag" you replied.
I don't know if you noticed how
quiet I went. I didn't dare speak.
It felt as if the Earth was breaking
up beneath my feet.
For so long, I had dreaded news
such as this. Time was up.
It's possible that my behaviour
struck you as a little odd, but
I kept staring out into the garden
because I couldn't face you
until I'd regained my composure.
I didn't want to alarm you.
There'd have been no point in that.
You were a little perplexed, I
know, when I turned and asked
if Billy had mentioned whether
the stag had spoken to him.
"What the fuck does that
matter?" you asked.
The white stag is Zeus.
It's one of his favourite guises.

He's used it many times before to destabilise me.
He shadows some accquaintance of mine in the knowledge that I'll get to hear about it.
Then he gradually steps up the mind-games, as he tries to make me unravel.
He will probably prance around playing Monarch of the Glen for a few more days. Then terrible things will start to happen.
But I'm not going to give him the satisfaction of seeing me panic. He's clearly intent on punishing me *yet* again, even if that means tormenting a vulnerable twelve year-old boy.
What kind of a Superior Being is that? Well I refuse to be intimidated by a hypocritical, bullying, nymph-shagging pervert.
I will set down my story so that it is told, and he is exposed as the empty, infantile braggart that he is.
Hopefully, that will put his nose out of joint. Perhaps. If he ever gets to find out. Actually, I'm not sure he would be bothered.

So, my Sunday got no better.
I spent most of the morning in a stunned daze. And then I found myself standing, still pretty befuddled, between two goalposts.

I was in no fit state to play. I should have lied and thrown a sickie. But I'd made a commitment to your brother.

The game began in a fine drizzle and it soon became clear that the opposition players were intimidated by my size. This was what I'd anticipated and, because they looked so spooked, I was expecting a quiet match.

Sure enough, every time I came out to gather a cross, or intercept a through-ball, they had the good sense to pull out of any physical challenge.

But there's always one, isn't there.

He had a reddened drinker's face and a cantilever belly. But in his fevered mind, he was Pelé. He lumbered through the mud, calling for the ball incessantly.
Every pass he played was a peach of a ball that his team-mate had been unable to reach because he was a

cunt/spazz/tosser/cripple (etc.)

Every free-kick he gave away was because the referee was a short-sighted prick/cheat/cheating prick.

He was an archetype. I've met hundreds of thousands of such individuals in my time — people who feel that their whole life is *someone else's fault*.

But this pot-bellied bigmouth was the most objectionable example I had seen in quite a while.

I sensed that he'd do, or try to do, something that was stupidly macho. And, sure enough, when one of our players hit a short back-pass, the oaf came trundling towards me. I picked up the ball on the edge of the penalty area and waited for him to decelerate.

But no, this moron wanted to late-tackle me, just to show everyone how hard he was. So he kept coming, with his right foot raised to rake my shin with his studs.

The crack was so loud that everyone stopped playing on the adjoining pitches.

I've heard countless bones breaking and that was certainly one of the most resonant.

As he lay in the mud, squealing like a pig in mid-slaughter and with his foot splayed outwards at ninety degrees, I saw the colour drain from your brother's face.

"Jeees-us, that does not look good" he winced, before phoning for an ambulance.

I suppose, if I'm honest, with hindsight, I could have taken evasive action. But I chose not to. Just as he made the choice to try and hurt me.

He can put this one down to experience.

It took some time to load him into the ambulance – in his view because the paramedics were "incompetent fucking wankers".

It's true that they did drop him off the stretcher at one point, but I'm not sure that was an accident.

It must have been nearly an hour before the match resumed and, as half-time drew near, I began to experience an unsettling sense of being watched.

I turned around to find a sturdy, glowering youth was standing behind the goal. It was young Billy Ballantyne. (And you're right. He is big for his age)

With his hands thrust deep into the pockets of his camouflage jacket and his shoulders hunched against the wind, he looked solitary and forlorn.

The dark hollows below his eyes suggested that he wasn't getting much sleep. Zeus's playthings never do.

I felt a deep sympathy for him – and a kinship of sorts. He had the air of a cornered animal.

His eyes kept darting to the ground in acute, self-conscious discomfort, as if he was ashamed of his thoughts.

Every now and then, almost imperceptibly, his head twitched.

(Have you noticed that? Or has he always done it?)

The lad was obviously struggling with many problems and, for a brief moment, I wondered if I'd let paranoia run away with me. Perhaps the white stag only existed inside his head.

Perhaps drugs had put it there.

I tried to make contact.

"Hiya Billy!" I called, with a cheery wave.

No response. Just a long look at the ground.

"How's tricks?"

Still nothing.

"Heard you've been having a wee bit of a hard time. Sorry about that."

He muttered something, darkly, as he stabbed at the mud with his foot.

"Sorry, didn't quite catch that" I said.

"Not supposed to talk to you" he mumbled, barely audible.

Cries of 'Malcolm!' warned me that the other team were on the attack. I turned around in time to gather up a half-hearted shot from a long way out. Then, after booting the ball upfield, I tried, gently, to quiz Billy. I didn't turn to face him, I wanted to avoid making him feel threatened.

"Who told you not to talk to me?" I asked, as casually as I could manage.

No answer. A plastic bag blew across the goalmouth. I scooped it up and walked around the back of the goal.

"Do me a favour, Billy, stick that in the bin over there, will you?"

He looked at me with a mixture of fear and hatred.

"OK, don't worry," I said, scrunching up the bag and tucking it into the corner of the net.

Billy stood behind the goal for a couple of minutes and I waited to start questioning him again. I'd need to pick my moment because he was transmitting a steady hum of hostility.

Then, from nowhere, he said "Where's my Dad?"

"Your dad?"

"Yeh, I don't see him. I'm supposed to be fetching the door-key from him. Has he been subbed already?"

It was actually quite a strong resemblance. All you had to do was imagine Billy's face encircled by pink fat.

I tried to break the news gently. I told him that his dad had been injured and was on his way to hospital.

Billy took a few kicks at the mud.

"Is it bad?" he asked.

"I think he'll be on crutches for a while"

He didn't seem overly concerned by the prospect.

The ref blew for half-time and the players started to drift towards the dressing-rooms. It felt like an opportunity for some privacy.

"Are you locked out without the key?" I asked. Again, no reply. He just kept glaring at me in short, snatched glances.

I decided to dive in.

"This is daft, Billy. Who told you not to talk to me?"

He looked up. The drizzle had lacquered strands of hair on to his forehead, which made him look oddly middle-aged.

I felt really sorry for him, Bessie, and I was trying to be sensitive, I really was. But my frustration took over.

"Was it the white stag?" I blurted out.

Billy scowled. "The doctors say the stag isn't real"

"You need to be careful" I said. Damn! That had come out sounding like a threat. I was getting this all wrong.

He'd started backing away from me now, but I persisted.

"The stag likes to trick people"

"No, that's *you*," he spat back "I know who you are, he told me, I *know*!"

The boy started to nod repeatedly, as if he was reassuring himself.

"This is a disguise. You're not Malcolm."

For a second, I wondered if the stag had told him my true identity.

"You're the Devil" hissed Billy.

The Devil? That was a new one. Zeus had obviously decided to have some fun with the Presbyterians.

"I'm not the Devil, Billy" I said, aware of sounding absurd. "You know me. You've seen me dozens of times, I'm the huge fella who lives with one of your teachers."

I took a small step towards him, but he bolted away across the playing fields, shouting and screaming that I was the Devil and that I'd get what was coming to me.

Nobody really paid him any attention. I suppose Sunday morning footballers are used to hearing threats and abuse.

For a moment, I considered catching him up and trying to explain. But where would I have begun, eh? He's twelve.

By the time your brother and his mates emerged for the second half, I was muttering to myself, cursing obscenely and profanely in ancient tongues that I'd not used for many, many centuries.

Ross looked a bit worried and asked if I was alright.

I told him that I was fine and dandy, which probably sounded like sarcasm. If I don't see him again – which is highly possible – can you apologise to him for me?

That's a setback.

I can hear you moving around in the kitchen.

I think you must have been woken up by Ralph McGeew's stupid bloody car alarm. When is he going to get that thing fixed? It's ludicrously over-sensitive. A leaf falls somewhere in Birmingham and half of the Highlands gets deafened.

I can't risk you coming up here and finding me doing this. So I'll lock this away, head downstairs and pretend that everything is normal and we're not being stalked by a psychopathic deity.

Yet again, my love, I'm so sorry about all the lying.

And I'm sorry that looks so pathetic written down.

I have no idea what just happened!
Where did that come from?
You went off like a firecracker!
I've been on this planet for
thousands of years and I can't
remember a more bewilderingly
sudden argument.
One moment we were having breakfast,
the next you'd stormed out!
I've been replaying the conversation
in my mind to try to pinpoint what
caused the fireworks.

You were telling me how you'd
been cornered by Mrs. Mendonca
– the human version of the Internet,
as you've often called her.
I was concentrating on trying
to appear normal, so mostly I
just listened and nodded.
You said that she'd asked
after me and, not for the first time, had
conjectured that I was a wizard
because I never seem to age.
Mrs. Mendonca had, apparently,
joked that I'd looked thirty
years old for the last twenty years.

(She's wrong. I've looked thirty years-old for several millenia)

If you recall, this prompted you to ask me what happens in forty years time, when you're 'a wizened old hag' and I look like 'your toyboy'.

For the record, Bessie, I didn't answer because I was upset. He won't let us have any future together. I didn't trust myself to respond.

I was not 'freezing you out'

Then, somehow, you hopped back to the subject of Mrs. Mendonca. It's possible you remember our conversation as vividly as I do, but I doubt that – you were pretty fired up.

You said she'd asked when I 'was going to make an honest woman of you'.

I said I was surprised she was so keen on marriage, given that her husband had faked his own death and turned up in Tasmania.

Normally, you'd have laughed. Not today. Things got a bit lively after that, didn't they Bessie?

I'd not slept, so that probably made me a wee bit over-sensitive. But you'd always given me the impression that you weren't bothered about getting married.

So I really wasn't expecting the accusation that I had allowed our relationship to 'just drift along with no sense of direction.'

"Isn't happiness a direction?" I asked. At which point, you went *absolutely* nuts and accused me of talking like a greetings card.

Well, yes, it *was* trite. But I was scared, especially when you started talking about kids.

So I shut the conversation down. I can see how that might have come across as provocative. I'm sorry. We don't normally talk about serious stuff over breakfast.

That was one hell of a slam you gave the front door.

They probably heard that in Dundee.

You called me a coward, Bessie. But, on reading this, I hope you'll understand why I was reluctant to discuss having children.

It makes me sad that you're angry with me. Especially as we have so little time left.

There's no point moping. I've got a story to tell.

My earliest childhood memory is of a day of bewilderment.

I must have been four or five years old. It was boiling hot and my brother and I were trying to catch lizards in the backyard.

Then my father appeared, in his General's uniform, and told my brother to go collect some lemons. I was told to follow my father inside.

It was plain that something was wrong because my mother was trembling and her face was taut with tension.

Typically, my father cut to the chase.

"Listen, Alceides, we've got some news to tell you and you mustn't get upset"

My brain started to race. I felt frightened. Were they going to send me away?

"The thing is..." he began "it's.. it's like this, I'm afraid that we're going to have to change your name."

I asked why. He glanced nervously at my mother.

"Because we've thought of a better name" he said. "Heracles. Fantastic name. Much better, much better."

I asked why it was a better name and was told it was better because it was a lucky name.

My parents repeated many times how lucky I was to have this new lucky name.

"Why is it lucky?" I asked.

My mother let out a sudden, weird laugh, as if someone had dropped ice down her back.

"Because it means 'glory of Hera'" she explained. "And Hera is the wife of mighty Zeus.... and it would be.. well, nice, if she felt.. positively towards you... as you grow up"

I asked my mother why Hera's positive feelings would be nice and she immediately collapsed into huge, gulping sobs.

Then she started pounding her chest with her fists. And wailing. One of the dogs started to howl in sympathy.

"I think that's enough questions for now" said my father, trying to make himself heard above the din. "Your name's changed. Just one of those things. It's nobody's fault."

I asked if Mother was going to be alright, because she was now banging her head against the wall and shrieking that she didn't deserve to live.

"She'll be fine, son. She's having a bad day, that's all, woman's stuff."

(Yes, sexist, but normal for Ancient Thebes)

I went for a walk in our olive grove and said my new name out loud, over and over again. It would take some getting used to, but I'd never really liked the name Alceides.

A few hours later, my father came and fetched me.

"We're making a sacrifice to Hera. Come. It's time you saw your first sacrifice."

I wasn't sure I wanted to see my first sacrifice.

The very word 'sacrifice' used to fill small children with dread because there were whisperings that to please the gods, sometimes, kids got thrown down wells.

Why the gods would want wet, dead children was a mystery to us. But, at that age, you presume that the adults must know what they're doing, don't you.

My father took me to the barn and picked out a dark brown cow which happened to be my favourite.

We led Mimosa (I'd named her that) across several hills until, finally, we climbed an extremely steep hill that was topped by a gleaming white temple.

Several masked priestesses rushed out to meet us and immediately began annointing Mimosa with various sacred and expensive oils.

She didn't seem to mind. She was a very gentle animal.

My father, meanwhile, was getting involved in a long, animated conversation with a woman I took to be the High Priestess, because she had the biggest mask.

I couldn't quite make out what was being said, but, every now and then, I'd hear my father exclaim "How much?"

Once their conversation was over, the

High Priestess led Mimosa towards an altar that was decorated with some very bloodthirsty friezes.

"Can we go, please?" I asked.

"No, son. We have to bear witness. It's part of the act of worship."

Then, all the Priestesses began some discordant chanting, as the High Priestess proceeded to slaughter Mimosa with a combination of brutality and incompetence.

It seemed to take forever.

My father and I watched this butchery, in searing heat, until the Priestesses ceased their wailing and the High Priestess walked away from the carcass.

"Well, that's that," said my father. "Worth doing."

Then he took my hand and led me down the hill, muttering that it was always best to be on the safe side.

From that day forwards, I was Heracles.

Overnight, all the children of Thebes, including my brother, seemed to switch to calling me by my new name.

It was as if an edict had gone out.

It became harder for me to get friends to come and play at my house. Everyone seemed wary around me.

Still, it didn't matter, I told myself. I had my brother to play with and an endless supply of new toys – like most kids with guilt-ridden parents.

As the years passed, I grew away from the other children in every sense. By the age of eleven, I stood well over six feet tall, with a broad chest and the thick thighs of an athlete.

I had to get used to being stared at, or, at least, I had to get used to hiding the fact that it bothered me.

On my twelfth birthday, my father – back from his latest military campaign – took me to a nearby beach.

We chatted about a whole range of topics, which was unusual and I sensed he was gearing up for something.

After we'd been sitting there for a few hours, he went quiet. Then I heard him take a deep breath. Something was definitely coming.

"Do you know where babies come from?" he asked, rather suddenly.

Confidently, I told him that I did know. And to prove it, I drew a diagram in the sand.

My father peered at it for a few moments.

"Yes, that's roughly it" he said. "Apart from the dragon."

I explained that I'd only added the dragon to show him how good I'd become at drawing dragons.

"Right, Heracles, well, um, the..er the.. process that you've drawn there that's..that's the least important part of being a father. The important bit is what follows. All..all the love..and the.."

His voice tailed off as he stared into the sand.

It wasn't like him to be nervous and searching for the right words. He was famous for his stirring speeches that sent men into battle.

But now he was tongue-tied and it made me feel frightened.

"The thing is, son" he began "Um,

it's.. well, what happened was... I was.. when you were.. see, I was away, fighting our enemies. And your mother was at home, waiting. That's not an easy thing, waiting."

He was staring even more relentlessly into the sand now.

"Anyway.. imagine how thrilled your mother was when she got word that victory was mine and that I was on my way home. So, that night, when I turned up at the house, safe and sound, she took me off to the bedroom and.. well, you were made."

He stopped staring into the sand and looked up.

"Only... that wasn't me"

He paused to take a deep, tremulous breath.

"The man looked and sounded exactly like me. But that was Zeus."

He stopped for another calming breath.

"I returned home the following night. Your mother and I had a few puzzling conversations, but I just presumed she'd been knocking back the barley wine. So, y'know.. we went upstairs and ..made a baby. Your brother. But, of course, when we had twins we naturally assumed that we had made both of you.. the normal way"

I wanted to ask questions, but there seemed to be a rock lodged in my throat.

My father squeezed my arm affectionately.

"It's a shock, I know. It was a shock for us when old Tiresias explained what had happened. The day we decided to change your name."

He explained that Tiresias was a seer; blessed with the gift of seeing the unseeable deceptions of the gods.

"But what if this Tiresias is wrong?" I stammered, as the tears started to roll down my cheeks before dropping onto the sand.

"No, no, no, Tiresias is never, ever wrong. He knows everything. He's the one who told us to change 'Alceides' "something that might... find favour with Hera. She's well-known for persecuting the offspring of her husband's... adventures."

I was far too young to challenge such mumbo-jumbo. But I was old enough to know when something was just plain wrong. Zeus had tricked my mother!

My father just shrugged.

"He's a God. They play by different rules"

Then he embraced me, something he did very rarely.

"But you'll always be my son" he said, with a wee catch in his voice. "This changes nothing"

But it did, Bessie. It changed everything. Our relationship began to deteriorate from that moment, I still can't quite explain it. It quickly got to the stage where the sound of his voice would irritate me beyond belief.

My relationship with my mother also worsened, though there'd never been much chemistry between us.

She was a woman who struggled to control her emotions, but never for very long.

Mostly, she just surrendered to them,

letting them fling her around like a rag doll.

To be fair, she was hardly unique. Most Greek noblewomen had a flair for drama. Perhaps that wasn't surprising, given that they had nothing to do.

Servants looked after the house, nurses cared for the children, what did that leave? There was embroidery, and there was looking beautiful, and there was waiting for your husband to return from battle, or a sea-journey, or some other great, male enterprise.

It's little wonder that women like my mother binged on their own emotions. They were staring into an abyss of pointlessness, like so many aristocratic wives over the centuries.

Increasingly, I found her to be an embarassment.

Every time I went out she'd bombard me with her fears, always reminding me how special I was and how being special carried risks.

Funny, isn't it, you say that almost every parent you meet nowadays will tell you that their child has been classified as 'special' and needs extra attention. Well, my mother was one of those parents. Teachers would hide when she approached.

Now, of course, I understand and accept that her love for me meant that she was always beside herself with worry.

But, back then, I was young and stupid.

Worse than that, I was young and stupid and I was huge. And to cap it all, I had been told I was the son of a God.

That could only mean trouble. I know that you've had to deal with dozens of horrible kids in your time, my love, but you've never taught one as obnoxious as I was. Trust me, I was in a league of my own.

To begin with, people were prepared to give me the benefit of the doubt. The consensus was that I was too young to fully understand my own strength.

That was why a badly-aimed discus sank a fishing boat, and

why an overthrown javelin impaled our neighbour's pig.

Gradually, however, everyone came to realize that I did know my own strength and was more than happy to abuse it. It was fun for me to casually lob people into dung-heaps, or push over horses for a bet.

At school, unfortunately, I was cheered on by a group of boys who I mistook for friends.

These hangers-on applauded every oafish prank and, to my eternal shame (literally!), I let them egg me on as I bullied a class-mate.

His name was Pelobus. He was a sickly-looking, stick-thin lad whose thoughts always seemed to be somewhere else.

He was socially awkward, partly because he had an awful stammer which was at its most excruciating whenever he tried to sound the letter 'p'.

I'm ashamed to say that, to entertain my 'fans', I'd often dangle Pelobus out of the window by his ankles and demand that he shout out his own name – something that, as he grew more terrified, became almost impossible for him. Quite often, he would vomit.

One morning, Pelobus didn't come to school. I never asked myself where he'd gone because he didn't matter to me. I never saw him again.

I told you, I was obnoxious.

Now though, thousands of years later, I can still picture his scared, ashen face. And I wonder what happened to him. And how his life turned out.

Only one of my teachers thought I was teachable.

He was a young Minoan called Enrolpus. I've no idea what he saw in me. Perhaps he just felt sorry for me. But, whatever the reason, he made me feel like I wasn't a freak.

Enrolpus taught Music – taught it well – and he gave me one-to-one tuition on the lyre. Those lessons became the highlight of my week. For one hour, it felt like my life belonged to me.

There was another teacher who stands out in my memory.

His name was Linus. He was a seedy scrag-end of a man.

Everything about him looked half-finished. He had a lazy eye, a wispy suggestion of a beard and, for some reason, he *absolutely loathed* me.

He always singled me out, but things really started to get out of hand in Middle School when I joined his class for Literature.

You wouldn't ~~appr~~ approve of his teaching style; it was mostly built around mockery.

He called me 'Muscles' and liked to caricature me as a lumbering blockhead.

Once, I arrived a few minutes late for his class – though I was not the last.

"Nice of you to pop by, Muscles" he drawled, with his trademark smirk.

I explained that I'd lost track of time, practicing the javelin out on the games-field.

"Ah yes," he pouted. "The javelin. Such a noble pursuit. And tell me, did you manage to throw it a long way?"

I told him that I'd thrown it a very long way.

He threw up his arms in mock surprise.

"A *very* long way! My, my! And did the pointy bit stick in the ground? Do tell, Heracles."

I didn't bother to answer.
He raised his voice to make one of his proclamations.
"The javelin.. is an example of a paradox. Why is it a paradox?
...anyone?"
The entire class stared at him in indifferent silence.
"Because it has a point.. but is also..pointless."
He beamed smugly for a moment, but nobody laughed so he lost his temper.
I was told to stay after school and sweep every dead leaf from the playing fields.
There were many such petty acts of vindictiveness. Luckily, I had my solo lessons with Emolpus to maintain my morale. He became my friend as well as my teacher.
The months limped past and I dreamt of the day when I'd be old enough to go and fight the hated Minyans alongside my annoying father and his regiments of hand-picked, broken-nosed men.
Then, one morning, I was sitting in the Music Room waiting for Emolpus, when in walked Linus.
"I'm taking you for music today" he said.

I asked where Encolpus was.
"Gone" said Linus. "Half the Academy funds had gone missing and they found the money under his bed. Anyway, he's made a run for it. You won't be seeing him again."
I struggled to take all this in for a few moments – and then I burst into tears.
I felt abject; my only real friend was gone and here I was stupidly humiliating myself in front of my worst enemy.
But, to my amazement, I heard Linus say "You cry as much as you need to. There's no shame in that. Even the sons of gods are allowed to cry."
For a moment, I wondered if he was being sarcastic. But when I looked up, he was smiling with a gentleness I'd not seen before. Linus said we'd skip today's lesson, as I'd had such a shock.
He suggested that I go for a walk by the river.
"I find that helps sometimes" he said.
The next few weeks were difficult, as I tried to come to terms with the

idea that my friend had turned out to be a thief.

But the Music Lessons were a pleasant surprise. Linus, I discovered, was a fine musician and a good communicator.

Better still, he was happy to make the time for me to discuss my feelings.

We talked about my distress concerning Emolpus, my self-consciousness about my size, my discomfort about my notoriety and my increasing detachment from my parents.

It all poured out of me. And he just listened.

The change in Linus was remarkable and I felt very guilty that I had so misjudged him.

After a few months, he'd become as good a friend to me as Emolpus. I felt very easy in his company.

One morning, out of the blue, he asked if I believed that Zeus really was my father.

I replied that I wasn't sure what I believed.

"I don't believe in Zeus!" he exclaimed, so suddenly that he almost seemed to have surprised himself.

He inched closer and lowered his voice.

"I don't believe in any of the gods. They're just stories conjured up by man to explain the things that scare him"

I said that he could well be right. After all, even though we were supposed to be related I had never once seen or heard Zeus.

"Of course you haven't!" Linus hissed. "A lot of the enlightened men of Thebes think as I do. We've formed a Secret Society"

He carried on, excitedly, as I sat re-tuning my lyre.

I noticed that his voice kept rising in pitch, almost as if someone was tuning him.

"The gods are history now" he declared "Man is god. And the bond between men is civilization. The mutual respect, the thirst for shared knowledge, shared experience"

I told him that I found his ideas appealing, as I hunted for some resin. Behind me, Linus continued laying out his free-thinking manifesto.

When I turned around he was naked.
Stark naked.
I asked him what the hell he was doing and told him to put his clothes back on immediately.
But he didn't. He just stood there.
"Do you have any idea what obcession feels like?" he asked, with a strange wobble in his voice.
Again, I told him to put his clothes on.
"It's torture" he wailed. "I've loved you from the first moment I saw you. And I think.. dare to think.. that perhaps you've grown to love me too"
It occurs to me, Bessie, that you may be finding this hilarious, your Malcom being propositioned by a naked man.
Well, for your information, hundreds of men have made passes at me. But Linus was the first, and I was very young and way, way too inexperienced to laugh it off.
At that age, you take everything so seriously — including yourself.
Unsure of how to react, I decided that I would let him down as gently as I could.
I valued Linus's friendship — I told him that — and he smiled. Then I told him that I profoundly

admired him. But I did not love him in that way.

"But you could!" he cried "Dare to love me, Heracles, dare!"

Calmly, and politely, I told him that I didn't feel the need to dare.

"I love you!" he proclaimed, stepping closer.

"Well that's.. very sweet" I said, looking away from his pale radish of a body. "But what you call love is just a passing.. crush that–"

"How can you say that?" he shrieked, drowning out my attempt at calm reason. "Of course it's real love! I love you so much I'd risk everything! I've already risked so much. How do you think that money ended up beneath Emolpus's bed!"

I felt my pulse suddenly quicken. Linus stuck out his scrawny sparrow's chest.

"I'm not ashamed of it."

A wave of nausea swept over me, as Linus boasted of how he'd viewed my love for Emolpus as an obstacle. So he'd planted the money.

Then he told Emolpus that it would be futile for him to stay and try to prove his innocence. They'd hang him from the Tree of Thieves.

"So he *ran*" he said, relishing the words. "Ran like a dog. But if he'd *really* loved you, as I do, he would never have been able to leave. *Never!*"

By now, I could hear a relentless thumping in my temples and I could feel my face getting hotter – red-hot.

Linus was spreading his arms wide, as if siezed by ecstasy.

"Love guided my hands! Love is our destiny! We were fated to taste each other!"

The pounding in my brain had become deafening, like a thousand drums, and, in a split-second, I threw myself at Linus and struck him on the side of the head with the lyre!

He dropped instantly to the floor. Blood and brains were already starting to bubble out of the large hole in the left side of his skull.

I had killed my first man.

It all happened so quickly.

I didn't plan it. That's not an excuse.

I just need you to understand.

I can hear your key in the front door. That's unexpected.

I'm going to head downstairs and hope that you're no longer angry with me.

Well Bessie, that was good and bad.

The good bit was that we made up – in the nicest possible way.

The bad was when you showed me the vile text messages that Billy Ballantyne has started sending you.

37 of them! In one morning! You were remarkably phlegmatic about them. You certainly didn't let Billy spoil your lunch. You were right, of course, when you said that abuse on social media is par for the course now, even for teachers.

But this is different, my love. Billy is targeting you because he is being wound up by Zeus. The kid is an automaton. Zeus is ramping up the pressure on me by increasing the threat to you. He's making it clear that he expects me to move on now.

So that's why I was making 'that face'.

And it's why I told you to notify the police and to make sure that you never found yourself alone with Billy. And it's why I was so keen to accompany you back to school.

I wanted to keep an eye on you. But I suppose I should have known that you would laugh it off and call me a drama queen.

In the end, I decided not to press the matter because I didn't want to frighten you.

I could sense that, deep down, you were a wee bit rattled, even though you said you weren't going to be intimidated by a kid who couldn't spell 'whore'.

After you left, I rang Ronnie McVey and asked him to keep a discreet watch on you. I hope he hasn't been creeping you out.

Sorry. I was worried.

Back to Thebes.

Don't worry, Bessie, I know you don't like people who blether on about how terrible their childhood was.

This won't be a Mis-Mem. But my youth is where I was ~~shaped~~ mis-shaped.

My parents hired a top defence lawyer called Xylopraxes. He was short, fat and festooned in chunky, clattering jewellery. His face was dyed with berry-juice and his hair was a shiny purple. But, in Thebes, that passed for style.

Once he'd heard my account of the killing, Xylopraxes started to think out loud.

"Provocation," he said "that's our best bet"

My father agreed. It seemed like a solid defence.

I pointed out that Linus had made sexual advances; for a man to force his attentions on a young boy -well, that had to be unacceptable behaviour, surely?

Xylopraxes looked at me.

"This is Greece" he said.

After some pacing and muttering, the lawyer suddenly jabbed a chubby finger in the air.

"Linus denied the existence of the gods! And you were outraged by his blasphemy!"

My father nodded in approval as Xylopraxes grew more excited.

"So, any right-thinking citizen in your position would have struck the heretic with that lyre!"

The lawyer's voice got louder and deeper.

"And..and, not appeciating your own strength, what you meant to be an admonishing tap turned out to be a skull-cleaving blow!"

I'd have preferred to cite the provocation that Linus had framed my friend; that, at least, had the advantage of being true. But the lawyer dismissed it as impossible to prove.

"The blasphemy angle is a surefire winner," he said. But he was wrong.

Justice is shaped by atmosphere. On the day my case came to court, the preceding trial involved five privileged young men who'd also employed an expensive lawyer.

The lawyer explained to the panel of white-haired judges that the young men had beaten an inn-keeper to a pulp because they'd heard him profanely cursing the name of Zeus.

One judge immediately launched into a diatribe against 'youths' who refuse to take responsibility for their actions.

"Then they have the nerve to claim that they're acting on behalf of the gods - which is, itself, an act of heinous sacrilege!"

"There's too much of this sort of

thing," said another greybeard.

"I blame the parents" said a third. I noticed my father and Xylopraxes exchanging glances.

Twenty minutes later, the trial was over. All five guilty, punishable by death.

The judge who pronounced the sentence did so with all the usual relish of an old man passing judgement on the young.

There followed a pedantic legal discussion about the size of stones to be used in the stoning, and then the court adjourned for light refreshments.

Xylopraxes and my father bustled me into a quiet corner of the courthouse-thing. The lawyer said he was abandoning the blasphemy angle. Then he told me to try to look smaller and more vulnerable!

I know this all reads like some dark comedy, Bess, but I can assure you it didn't feel funny at the time. I was sixteen years old and it felt like the world hated me.

My trial began with an opening statement from Xylopraxes.

"Your justices, this boy is innocent"

he said, with a throwaway tone, as if he was simply correcting a small misunderstanding.
"He does not deny causing this man's death, nor does he claim to be acting in the name of the gods, no, no, that is not his defence"
Xylopraxes paused to create tension. I waited to hear what my new defence was.
"This... was an accident!" he boomed. "You cannot takes this boy's life!"
At this point, my mother became overwhelmed. She began to wail in the spectators' gallery. The judges had her immediately removed. No-one objected.
Once she had been carried out, flailing her arms, Xylopraxes began the case for the defence.
He explained that I had been, on the day in question, practicing a particularly difficult piece of music on my lyre.
In a moment of frustration, I had hurled my lyre at the wall. But my aim had not been true. He explained that - because of its shape - the lyre is a particularly difficult instrument to throw.
Tragically, my lyre had veered off to the side and then smashed

into my poor music teacher's head.

Is that it? I thought.

He can't be serious. He's going to get me killed.

But Xylopraxes had barely begun. For the next few hours, he treated the court to an extraordinary display of rhetoric and stagecraft.

At one point, he produced a melon, placed it on a rostrum and then threw a lyre at it.

He kept missing the melon, which he felt clearly demonstrated how the instrument was an erratic projectile.

Then he handed me the lyre. I understood what I had to do. I threw the lyre several times, taking care not to hit the melon.

"Y'see!" cried the lawyer. "That, my friends, is scientific evidence!"

He seemed to be winding up for a big finish. He turned a slow, full circle as he surveyed his audience.

"Heracles.." he paused, letting my name hang in the air for a moment "...did you deliberately throw that lyre at your music teacher?"

"No, sir" I replied, with the firmness of a liar.

Xylopraxes announced that he had no further questions and sat

down to applause from the spectator
on his payroll.

One of the judges raised a hand
and asked me the name of the pi
of music that I had found so very
maddening.

I hesitated, but Xylopraxes immedia
bobbed to his feet and said it wa
called 'An Air to Poseidon'.

"And what's so damned difficul
about it?" asked the judge.

"I believe it's what they call 'mo
lyre music'" the lawyer explained.

All the judges started mutterin
and shaking their heads.

Next, it was the prosecution's tur
Their lawyer was very lacklustre. H
questions were clumsy and the
traps he laid were obvious and
easily avoided.

He seemed to sense he was faili
so, in desparation, he threw the ly
at the melon in an effort to prove
that it was not so hard to throw
one with accuracy.

But instead he hit a vase, smas
it to pieces.

The judges looked on impassively.
"You'll have to pay for that" one
of them said.

Finally, the prosecutor summarised his case and sat down.
The judges asked Xylopraxes if he had anything further to add, with a reminder that it was nearly lunchtime.
Xylopraxes did have something to add. He rose to his feet and pointed out that I was of noble lineage, descended from Perseus.
"We're all descended from Perseus" called a voice from the crowd.
"Exactly!" cried the lawyer. "We are all sons of Perseus! All are equal! Equal before the law!"
He scanned the panel of judges. "Now.. I know that there are.. rumours, concerning my client's .... paternity."
A ripple of unease travelled across the courtroom.
" ...but that is of no relevance to us".
I glimpsed my father breaking into a sly smile, as if he'd been expecting the card that the lawyer was about to play.
"It is totally immaterial. What does it matter if the accused is, in some way, special to the

omniscient Gods? This case is being tried by men. Mortal men. *You*, my lords, must decide. And if you find Heracles to be guilty … then so be it…"

I felt panicky. What the hell was he playing at?

"…and any possible retribution from the gods, no matter how swift and terrible that might be… is a mystery that has *no* bearing on this case."

This time, Xylopraxes sat down to no funded applause, just an eerie silence.

Eventually, the judges went into a huddle and I felt the knot in my stomach tighten.

These half-dead old fools were about to decide whether I had a future.

In the front row of the gallery, two of Linus's brothers, were staring relentlessly at me.

To my eyes, the expressions of the judges looked alarmingly stern. But the word 'Zeus' did seem to be recurring in their whispers.

After what felt like an age—but was probably a few minutes—they cast their votes.

Seven pebbles were white, three black. Not guilty.

My father smiled and warmly shook my hand, as I fought desperately to not burst into unmanly tears.

Xylopraxes slapped us both heartily on the back as he handed my father his bill.

Amphitryon studied the numbers for a while.

"Looks like I'll have to sieze more herds off those Minyans" he said.

And so began the Twenty Years Cattle War.

That farce of a trial, Bess, triggered a terrible, disastrous change in my personality.

It fostered a sense that I was immune to the consequences of my actions.

I had killed a man.

Nothing had happened.

Clearly, I was special.

Life was going to be fun.

The general concensus in Thebes seemed to be that I was a spoilt rich boy who had got away with murder.

So I quickly started to sense some resentment. Especially when I got stabbed.

I know that, no doubt, you're appalled by the revelation that your Malcolm is a murderer, and a perjurer. Well I'm afraid there's worse to come.

Sorry, my love, but I feel I have to tell you everything. Isn't that strange? I've never felt like this before.

I could leave out the story of how I got stabbed, because I'm racing against the clock, so many episodes will have to be left out

But though the incident was quite banal, it was significant.

We were in the market. My mother was haggling with a stall-holder over the price of a nerve-tonic.

I was waiting, bored.

A man walked towards me, smiling. At first, I thought he'd punched me in the stomach and run away. But then I heard my mother scream and felt something dripping on to my feet, which I realized was my blood.

I had a punctured spleen — certain death, according to the family physician. So my mother demanded a second opinion.

The second doctor said my only hope was his new pioneering treatment, which would involve covering my entire body in large, African hornets.

Mother didn't hesitate, what mother would?

The hornet-stings were much more painful than the stab-wound, but, amazingly, I was back on my feet in less than a week.

My recovery was, of course, attributed to the hornet treatment, (The doctor made an absolute fortune) But I began to wonder if I'd received confirmation of having divine blood. It was an important shift in how I saw myself. I started to believe that I might be immortal.

Of course, all teenagers believe themselves to be immortal.

That's why they joy-ride through town centres at ludicrous speeds every Saturday night.

But they grow out of it – if they live long enough.

I, however, was not going to grow out of it any time soon. And my sense of indestructibility didn't just make me reckless, it also made me loud and even more insufferably arrogant.

Again, I know this sounds nothing like the man you've known for 20 years but my sense of being exceptional was bending and twisting my mind.

My father decided that I should leave Thebes because it was full of people who wanted to stab me.

Linus's family were quite wealthy and it was rumoured that they'd hired teams of assassins.

So I was packed off to a distant cousin who owned a farm on the plain of Alenzaria.

It was barely a farm – just a few acres of scrub that provided the grazing for a herd of ridge-backed, very stupid oxen.

The plain could not have been more plain. It seemed virtually featureless, apart from the odd thorn-bush.

Every now and then, a sneaky wind would throw a handful of dust in your face.

I hated the place. It was a total dump with not the slightest bit of excitement – unless you counted the lions.

At first glance, the lions were quite

impressive, but as soon as you shouted in their direction they would run away. Experience showed that these lions were a passive, cowardly bunch.

But there's always one, isn't there.

I never even heard him coming. I was peeing in the dust, making patterns, when suddenly I was smashed in the back and the ground leapt up and hit me in the face.

It was a massive shock. I'd never been knocked down before! Never. Not even as a child.

Immediately, I felt the pain as the lion's teeth drilled into my shoulder. I was in big trouble and whatever I was going to do had to be done quickly.

Somehow, I managed to flip over and grab its mane – to control the head and protect my throat. The creature's breath was foul and a dollop of scalding lion-spittle blurred my vision, but pure instinct had taken me over now.

I grabbed the jaws and started steadily forcing them further and further apart, wider and wider, until – at last – I heard the crack of a jawbone splintering.

The courage drained out of the creature in an instant.

It would have turned and ran. If I'd let it. But my blood was up.

One crashing punch to the head knocked it clean out and then I laid across the animal's throat, using my weight to crush its windpipe.

After a few minutes, it stopped breathing.

I stepped away and stared at it. The lion looked serene, almost as if it were sleeping.

Then, very suddenly, a wave of euphoria surged through me. I danced round the corpse, whooping and clapping and – for some bizarre reason – shouting my own name to the heavens.

I had ~~ha~~ killed a lion!

With my bare hands!

How many teenagers had done that? I was _so_ cool. That's how I thought. In that regard, at least, I was no different. I had the same priorities as every adolescent male on this planet.

I went back to the farm buildings, got my shoulder cleaned and bandaged, and then returned with a herdsman who I knew to be an expert skinner.

It took him less than half-an-hour to remove the whole lion-skin, head to claws.

I'd been intending to keep it as a rug, but instead I decided to wear it as a very showy cloak.

It was quite a fashion statement. The head formed a kind of hood, perched on top, so that I peeked out from beneath the top jaw — almost as if the lion had eaten me alive.

I felt it was very me.
You're always teasing me about my fashion sense (or lack thereof) but at least I no longer wear dead lions. You've got off quite lightly, my love.

In most versions of the legend, I fight two giant lions, with hides that are impenetrable to arrows.

Well, I did boast, far and wide, about my feat and I wore the lion-cloak to advertise my great heroism so, perhaps for once, I can't complain if the story-tellers got a wee bit carried away.

In case you're wondering, I don't think the Lion had anything to do with Zeus. During that phase of my life, I've got no evidence that the bastard was interfering in any way.

Sadly, each and every mistake was all my own work. Though I suppose he bears some responsibility because he afflicted me with my peculiar, distorting status.

Still, I could have tried harder to be less of a dickhead.

As Malcolm, I've tried very hard to be the opposite of a dickhead. I'm so sorry that I've gone and let you down now.

I would never have left you if I'd had a choice. No way.

After about a year of watching oxen, my father sent word that it was probably now safe for me to return to Thebes.

The murder of Linus had been overshadowed by more recent murders and Linus's family had pro[illegible]ised that they wouldn't [illegible]re any more people to stab me, provided my father compensated them with tons of money.

I was in no great rush to get home, so I decided to go the long way round and see a bit of the world. A gap year, basically.

It was during this period that I discovered I had a talent for languages.

Wherever I went, I found I was able to understand the locals very quickly. Usually, I was fluent within a month.

We had never studied foreign languages at school. Why would we bother? Thebes was clearly the centre of the universe.

You've often remarked on how good my French and Spanish are, but I actually know over 300 languages (though most of them are dead now)

I suspect that my gift may be inherited because Zeus is multi-lingual. When we were in Greece, he addressed me in Greek. In Carthage, he spoke Carthaginian. He will probably speak English soon.

The only place where I struggled to pick up the lingo was an island called Phryvacia which was inhabited by a tribe of sun-worshipping tongue-clickers.

You won't find Phryvacia in the history books. They fell prey to a cult of zealots who convinced them that their sun-god wanted them to incinerate themselves. So the entire population held hands and jumped into a very active volcano.

They left barely a single trace of their civilisation, although I have occasionally seen Phryvacian artefacts in museums, misattributed to cultures that historians have heard of.

My favourite language is Babylonian. (They had fourteen different words for 'slave') But my second favourite is English. It's so wonderfully bendy. It gives you so many choices.

I learnt my English while I was working on the trawlers out of Aberdeen in the 1930s.

So, that probably answers your question about why I can often sound a wee bit old-fashioned. (Still, that gave you one of your favourite jokes, eh Bessie? That I was born in black-and-white.)

The final stage of my journey home was a tedious ~~trek~~ trek through some hills which, as a child, had always looked distantly blue and alluring.

But now that I was actually trudging through them, they were decidedly brown.

To make matters worse, it would not stop raining, day after day, an incessant deluge.

On the third afternoon, as I reached the peak of the highest hill – probably a mountain by British standards – the path narrowed and grew more treacherous.

To my surprise I heard voices, male voices, through the drumming rain.

Some soldiers came marching around the bend, two abreast. The front pair stopped suddenly when they saw me.

In my lion-cloak, I must have presented quite a spectacle.

A man I took to be the commander

— because his helmet was covered in feathers — squeezed his way round them and approached me.

He seemed rather apprehensive. Behind him, came a Sergeant (no feathers). He was less apprehensive. He pointed at me and started laughing.

"Look, lads! It's a giant being shagged by a very thin lion!"

A few soldiers giggled, which I didn't appreciate, but I stayed civil, and I asked where they were from.

"We're from the North" replied the Commander, rather nervously.

"The North?"

"Yes," he said "The North".

Why was he so jumpy?

"We're headed for Messinas."

I pointed out that this was the road to Thebes.

"We're going via Thebes" he countered. "It's... a more interesting route"

They weren't from the North, they were Minyans. But I couldn't tell how many soldiers were around the blind side of the bend. Was it just a platoon? Or was it an army?

"Now, sir, if you wouldn't mind

letting us pass... only we are on a bit of a schedule"

He smiled at me. I smiled back. But I didn't budge.

"I must request that you step aside, sir" said the officer "that would be greatly appreciated... thank you"

The path was only wide enough for two and the drop was long and steep.

If I stood my ground, they couldn't advance. This raid - or whatever it was - would have to be delayed, or even abandoned.

"With respect, Captain, let's kill him" suggested the Sergeant.

"No killing will be necessary, Sergeant, I'm sure that this gentleman... I'm sorry, what's your name?"

I informed him that I was Heracles, son of Amphitryon.

The word 'Amphitryon' rippled back through their ranks. That was a name they feared.

The Sergeant stepped towards me. "Would that be Amphitryon the cattle-thief, rapist and murderer?"

I didn't bother to dignify that with an answer. I was in total control of the situation.

The path was <u>very</u> narrow and <u>very</u> slippery from the rain.
It would need a very brave soldier to get past me and, apart from the Sergeant, none of them looked like they had the stomach for it.
The officer certainly didn't.
"Alright men, about face!" he called, over the rattling of the rain.
This was perfect. The only alternative route would add days to their march. By then, I'd be back in Thebes and the city would be armed to the teeth.
Unfortunately, the Sergeant had worked this out.
"Sir, we can take him. We have over three hundred men."
Right, so it <u>was</u> an army.*
The officer repeated his order and the soldiers began to turn around.
"Heracles, yeh, I've heard of ~~you~~ you" said the Sergeant, walking towards me. "Didn't Zeus fuck your mother?"
"Sergeant!!" yelled the Captain "I said 'about face'!"
But the Sergeant kept walking towards me, with a swagger in his step.
"Yeh, that's right. Zeus fucked your mother. And she loved it. I heard that she moaned like a whore".

well Boss, you know how I feel about rudeness.

Logically, part of me knew that this trash-talk was an attempt to provoke me and that I should just ignore it.

But he had just insulted my Mum. So I hurled him over the precipice.

As his screams faded into the mist below, his comrades stared at me, open-mouthed.

I shouted "Boo!" and a couple of them dropped their spears. I was enjoying their terror. However, I was too young and stupid to realize that when human-beings are terrified they do not always run away.

The white-faced Captain raised his sword in the air and shrieked "Attack!"

He ran towards me, roaring.

I punched him in the face and he dropped down dead. He lay at my feet, staring up at me.

For a moment, I thought his men were about to take flight, as I could hear some anxious murmurings. But then a javelin whistled past my ear. And another. Now two soldiers were rushing at me, also shrieking

"Attack!"

The adrenaline had taken over now. I tore a shield from one soldier's grasp, as I stabbed him in the neck with my sword.

Then I used the shield to protect me from a hail of arrows. They had archers! What an idiot! Every army has archers!

Two arrows were already embedded in my thigh and more archers were scampering up the steep slope to my left.

I knew I was in trouble now, as I cleaved my way through the soldiers on the path. Some tried to turn and run, but the path behind them was blocked with men, so my sword hacked them down.

In all the noise and chaos, the beginnings of the landslide went unnoticed.

It began as a skitter-skatter of stones, dislodged by the feet of archers as they struggled to gain a footing.

But as I lashed out in every direction, I became aware that I was gradually sliding downwards. The entire hill was on the move!

Suddenly, the ground became the sky and I was flailing and tumbling in a rumbling avalanche of mud, rocks and screaming people.

I got fleeting glimpses of bodies getting buffeted and smashed by boulders.

An uprooted tree slid alongside me. Then a goat flashed past. Then a door. A chariot. A horse. A statue.

And still I was somersaulting! It felt like I would fall forever.

When it finally stopped, I found myself laying on top of a tangled heap of Nature.

I was battered and bruised, with two arrow-heads still stuck in my leg. All around me, twisted bodies – or bits of bodies – were poking out of the mud and rubble.

It was deathly quiet, apart from the hissing of the drizzle.

There was only one other survivor, a tiny, dazed Minyan archer who I found hiding beside a flattened barn.

Amazingly, there wasn't a scratch on him. But his body-shape looked wrong. When I lifted him to his feet, he cried out in pain and I realized that he'd broken his shoulder.

I asked if he was fit to walk and the boy muttered something and nodded.

He asked if he was my prisoner now.

"I suppose you are" I replied.

"So... will I be executed?" he mumbled.

I told him no, I would take him as my slave.

He wiped away a tear. "Promise?" he asked.

I gave him my promise.

The lad was tough. As we walked to Thebes, he never once complained about the pain that was etched on his face.

Our arrival in Thebes drew quite a crowd and, as we approached the palace, the soldiers of the royal guard encircled everyone.

King Creon always got jumpy when crowds started to gather.

The King emerged and immediately made the boy kneel before him.

"What was your mission, dog?" he sneered, aiming a limp kick at the hostage.

Even though the lad was only a few years younger than me, I felt protective towards him. I moved closer. In case things turned nasty.

In a barely audible croak, the boy said their mission had been to attack Thebes.

The King shook his head and addressed the crowd.

"My fellow Thebans! This is why we must put aside our differences, to unite against the terror from outside!"

The audience were unimpressed, but Creon pretended not to notice.

"So, dog, what reward were you promised?"

The boy mumbled that they'd been promised a strip of land for every pair of Theban ears.

A few spectators gasped in shock.

"So, dog, you'd have taken our ears, eh? But you were no match for this heroic son of Thebes. How many Minyans did you slay, noble Heracles?"

I opted for false modesty.

"A few," I said.

The boy lifted his head.

"It was more than a few. He fought like a hundred men. He knocked our soldiers off that pass like they were skittles."

Creon spread his arms ridiculously wide and boomed to the crowd. "Truly the gods have sent us a hero who out-heroes all of the heroes!"

I knew this was bullshit, but part of me was enjoying the attention. With appropriate modesty, I pointed out that the landslide had killed most of the Minyan army.

"Ex-actly!" exclaimed the king. "Even Mother Earth herself fights at your side!"

He spread his arms even wider. "This can only mean one thing, citizens of Thebes, the gods are smiling on their champion, Heracles!"

The crowd began to cheer. "And the gods are smiling on the Thebes.. of King Creon!"

The cheering stopped. Instantly. A few courtiers began some very polite applause – the kind you hear at Lords when a foreigner scores a boundary.

The King slowly scanned the assembly, as if making a private note of every face. He shouted the word 'Rejoice!'

Then he declared that a games would be held in my honour.

The crowd immediately started cheering again. A games meant a three-day public holiday.

Creon put his hand on my shoulder. "We'll send for your father. He's off retrieving cattle from some outlaws."

Something in the King's tone felt like a criticism, but it didn't bother me. I was too busy basking in all the ~~attention~~ adulation

The King announced that, as a celebration, he was distributing free wine to all citizens, and then he threw in a tax-cut for slave-owners.

The crowd went mad. I was engulfed by back-slapping fans.

I was so thrilled with my ovation that I didn't register the King shouting a decree that the poor, broken-shouldered boy should be sacrificed to Hera.

I didn't notice him being led away. By the time I got to hear about it, it had already happened.

Later, I heard that the Priests had made a horrible mess of the sacrifice. If Hera *does* exist, that won't have pleased her very much.

OK. It's now twenty past six and I'm sorry that I just rang you but I was worried; you were late home and you hadn't responded to my text.

I had completely forgotten it was Parents Evening and yes, you're right, it is written on the wall-calendar.

Hopefully, on reading this, my behaviour will make more sense. I can't help but be concerned about you, Bess

I also took the liberty of phoning P.C. Fraser and mentioning the vicious texts from Billy Ballantyne.

I know you thought it best to ignore them, but I just thought the police should be made aware.

By the time you get to read this, any danger will have passed. Once I move on, Zeus will leave everyone alone.

So, Creon – as you'll have guessed – was a ruler who was in trouble and I represented a feelgood factor.

But what did I care if, every time

I received a standing ovation, the King materialized right alongside me?

And if he commissioned friezes of me slaughtering Minyans, with his face smiling down at me – or even with him fighting alongside me, in a chariot pulled by centaurs – why should I worry?

It worried my father though. He felt I was allowing myself to be used. Mother just kept wailing.

But I wrote them off, they were old; old people worry. You can't let it stop you having a good time, every teenager knows that.

Besides, I was special, their advice didn't apply to me.

The 'Glory To Heracles Games' became a repeat event, every month. I took the gold medal, always, in every contest and once I even won a novelty race against a horse.

(No, my love, that's not bullshit, I beat a horse.)

I'd become a legend. It became hard for me to walk down the street. Fans camped on the grass outside our house. Lion-coats were everywhere.

They were being sold at stalls throughout Thebes, all owned – as it happened – by Xylopraxes the lawyer.

Demand became so great that he paid teams of archers to kill and skin every lion they could find.

Within a few years, there was not a single lion to be found until you reached Africa.

As my fame increased, I got free clothes, free food, free wine, free money.

And the more money I received, the less I paid for.

The money I lost gambling was invariably returned to me. I was given cattle, houses, all sorts.

I don't feel comfortable telling you about the sex, so let's just say there was a lot of it.

Every day women threw themselves at me, including the Queen.

It was Paradise for a seventeen-year-old boy (though physically I was far from a boy).

Sometimes, the women were even pimped by their husbands! It gave me quite a distorted view of sexual relationships.

My father disapproved. He told me I'd get diseases, which I did, but they'd

all clear up within a few days.
(Sorry, Bess. I know, too much information)
Amphitryon was also worried that I might be spawning lots of children.
Again, I wasn't bothered.
He was concerned, I think, that I might breed children with Zeus-like abilities and traits – more freaks like me, basically.
But I didn't really see a problem with that. I was happy to pass on my specialness.
As it turned out, word never reached me of any children that I might have casually sired during this reckless period of my life. As far as I'm aware, I fatherered no prodigious sons or daughters.
My only children – the children of my marriage – they were mortal.
But I'm getting ahead of myself.
And that's part of my story that I may not be strong enough to write.
So, there I was, footloose and apparently indestructible. A party animal, oblivious to any warnings, completely self-absorbed (or as you'd say 'up myself')

One weekend, I took my brother and several new best friends to a coastal resort, where we worked our way through all the local taverns.

Unsurprisingly, I can't remember much about it. But I do remember the morning we left.

As we packed up, my brother seemed in a very strange mood. He was watching me with intensity. And he was not talking, not a word, just watching. It was very unsettling. He was making me feel like an exhibit in a zoo.

Eventually, he said something. "I don't think you should drink. I.. I don't think you're cut out for it."

Well, I just laughed. I felt that I was very cut out for it.

"No, seriously" he interrupted "you ...when you've had a lot, I mean, an awful lot.. with no warning, you change." His voice tailed off. "You.. you turn into someone else."

"Isn't that the whole purpose of getting drunk?" I laughed.

He was staring at me with even more intensity now.

"You don't remember any of it, do you?"

I had no idea what he was on about.

"You sank several bottles of wine... and then you.. your face sort of collapsed.. your eyes went dead.. and you accused me of being your enemy"

I laughed in disbelief. He was winding me up, surely, the way that brothers do.

"You said I was an assassin, sent to kill you. But you were going to kill me."

His face had gone white as he relived the experience.

"So I ran, Heracles. Into the woods.. because you wanted to kill me".

I had no idea how to respond. I didn't remember any of this. I suggested that maybe the wine had been on the turn, or perhaps someone had spiked it.

Usually, I was an affectionate drunk.

Because my brother looked so scared I promised to cut down on the booze.

"I'm not sure I really like the stuff."

Not really. I only drink to be sociable"

"Yeh.. well, threatening to murder someone isn't very sociable" he said with a grim chuckle.

"No, it isn't". I ruffled his hair. "Forgive me, brother, I'm sorry."

And I was sorry. That was the last conversation we had. A few weeks later, by the cruellest of ironies, he got stupidly drunk and was killed in that ridiculous argument about triangles.

Quite often I find myself thinking about Xantes and the warning he gave me.

What he said, of course, was hugely significant and I should have listened to him. But I'm afraid I never took him very seriously. That's what happens with siblings, isn't it. You never heed Ross's advice, do you.

I can't say that I let my brother's death cramp my style. The parties continued, the invitations kept coming and Creon kept pursuing his agendas. One was matchmaking. He never failed to point out that I should take a bride and that he had a lovely daughter.

Politely, I'd point out that his lovely daughter seemed to despise me.

"Oh that's all part of the dance," he said "women love to pretend they despise you. I've seen it so many times."

He nodded as he remembered the 'dances'.

"Sometimes they even beat you with their fists, or run away. One threw herself down a well, the little minx"

(They were very different times, Bessie) The King was constantly engineering meetings between me and his daughter, Megara, but they always seemed to end with some waspish exchange.

She gave off a definite air of disapproval.

I don't think it helped that I was screwing her mother. (No, I'm not proud of it, I was seventeen, that's my defence)

Anyway, it felt like Megara

never missed an opportunity to dish out the vitriol.

One exchange sticks in my mind, I don't know why.

She began by asking if I was worn out from all my recent 'exertions'.

Here we go, I thought.

"I understand the judge's wife, Xylantha, is your latest penis-harbour" (nearest equivalent translation)

The important thing was to stay cool. I was determined not to let this woman get under my skin.

"I don't think it's any of your concern, is it? What goes on between two consenting adults?"

"Hm..." she considered "interesting use of the word 'adults'"

Then she swanned off to talk to one of the servants.

All my earliest memories of Megara involve her gliding away from me. She had the most expressive back I ever saw.

Still, what did I care?

So she didn't like me, so what?

She was just one woman. She was nothing special.

That's what I told myself.

A few weeks after that encounter, I was invited to yet another royal orgy. I was beginning to tire of these affairs, mainly because the Queen kept jumping me in the corridors. It was never a particularly pleasant experience. She had extremely long fingernails and a kiss like a hoover.

But I didn't want to reject her because - well, I just felt it probably wasn't a good idea to reject a Queen.

Anyway, I was hiding in a side-room when the King appeared and invited me into his private chambers, where the floor seemed to be carpeted with naked girls in various stages of narcotic stupor. (Relax, Bess, this bit isn't about sex.)

Creon sat me down in a corner and started to explain that Thebes had a major crisis on its hands.

His network of spies had told him that the Minyans were developing a new, huge and highly destructive kind of catapult which, clearly, they were planning to use against us.

The weapon could demolish our walls - probably in less than one hour. We needed to defend ourselves by attacking them.

"This must happen immediately," he said, "and I'm placing the entire army under your command."

"Why me?" I asked. "My father is the Commander"

Creon flapped his hands as if he was being pestered by flies.

"Yes, yes, yes.. but you're the invincible one. The Minyan soldiers will piss themselves when they see you."

I was flattered, but I declined - in that way that people decline when they don't want to appear too keen.

"You're worried about supplanting your father" said the King, "that does you great credit. You're a fine son"

He lowered his voice.

"But we have to face facts. Your father is growing old. He talks about the past all the time. He frets. He hesitates. Last month, I suggested a

punitive raid against ~~those~~ those bastard
Teleboans and he said he didn't
think it was feasible! Not feasible?
The old Amphitryon would have been
back with a sackful of Teleboan
noses and ears before you could say
'barley cake'."

He could sense that I was ripe for
the plucking. He spread his arms
wide and bellowed "You, son of
Amphitryon, can out-Amphitryon
Amphitryon!" (Yes, he really did
talk like that, Bess. Kings don't get
told when they're overdoing it)

Well, there are no excuses. I
suggested joint-command — but
I didn't mean it.

Looking back, my naivety makes
me cringe. Creon's popularity had
been plummeting. Only a few days
earlier, a citizen had stood on a
box in the market-place and
advocated a new form of government,
with no Kings, just elected representatives.
Creon had invited the man into
the Palace to discuss his interesting
new concept. The man had not been
seen since.

If I'd been paying a bit more
attention to politics (and indeed my
family) I'd have realised that my

father was now one of Creon's biggest critics. He'd been calling for an audit of the royal accounts, so the King was looking to marginalise him. But I understood nothing of this. So I let Creon play me like a harp.

A public proclamation followed, in which Amphitryon was thanked for all his years of public service and I was installed as the new General.

Deep down inside, I was excited by the profane thrill of supplanting my father.

The demotion shattered him. He was not surprised by Creon's strike – he had been expecting something – but he was stunned that I'd agreed to replace him. He lost weight, his face hollowed, he became a spectre sitting in his favourite chair.

We never talked about it. But his ghostly stare told me that he regarded me as a traitor.

For my part, I felt there was something pathetic about the way he'd just accepted defeat. Creon was right. My father had got old.

My mother was, as always, inconsolable. But this time, her anguish was edged with rage. How could I do this to my father? The distress would kill

him and I would be his murderer'.
But, to me, she had become no more than background noise.
The Minyan campaign was a walkover. Everything that Creon's spies had reported turned out to be wrong.
There were no giant catapults, no giant anything; just a small army of teenage conscripts.
Wearing my lion-cloak and armed with a specially-forged, armour-cleaving sword, I charged into their ranks with merciless ferocity.
The first battle was only a few minutes old when it became clear that this was already a rout.
Clear, that is, to any objective eye. But I was in the seething heart of the massacre, intoxicated by my own power.
So when the terrified Minyans held their arms aloft in surrender I ignored the signal and kept scything through their lines, mowing men as if they were corn.
My soldiers followed on behind, harvesting from the dead.
300 dead Minyans was the score,

but Creon almost certainly inflated that figure for propaganda purposes.

So not three hundred then, but I know that I ended many lives that day – and devastated many more.

The site of the carnage was a barren plain, broken up by impressive tooth-like rocks. The locals called it 'The Crone's Mouth'

A few months ago, I caught a glimpse of it on TV.

An empty-headed, cheerful presenter was touring the area as part of a holiday programme As he charged around in a land-cruiser saying 'wow' repeatedly, I went cold with revulsion.

No-one should holiday there. It's a cursed place. I saw to that.

I'm not coming out of this very well, am I?

The man you've loved, for so many years, turns out to be guilty of murder, infanticide and war-crimes.

Again, I don't know what to say. Perhaps the only way for both of us to get through this is to regard the young Heracles as a completely

different individual to Malcolm Galbraith.
(In a way, he is)
I was someone else back then, someone
I barely recognise. Someone who
hadn't yet learnt how to shudder.

Creon's popularity was boosted
by the 'victory' over the Minyans.
The people of Thebes were no brighter
than I was.

They came out in their thousands
for the triumphal games, which
this time featured battles
between slaves and huge Icarian
bears (also extinct now)

By this time, I had bought my
own house, with extensive gardens
full of fruit trees.

One morning, as I ate breakfast
on my balcony, a servant reported
that Amphitryon had turned up
at the perimeter gate.

It was the first time he'd visited
my house, and I wanted to show
it off. But he turned down my offer
of breakfast. He didn't want any
food.
He didn't even want to sit down.

"Is it true?" he asked.

"Is what true, father?" I replied. I genuinely couldn't guess what he was referring to.

"..That the Minyan troops were trying to surrender. But you just butchered them regardless."

I told him that I'd done my duty, which was to protect Thebes.

I had taken no prisoners, that was true, but the Minyans would not have spared anyone either - if they had been the victors (probably not the case)

And I pointed out to my father that he himself was renowned for his ruthlessness in battle.

"Yes, in battle" he snapped. "Not in victory."

I reminded him about the sackfuls of ears and noses.

"Those men had already died in combat" he protested. "It was just a way of keeping tally."

I laughed, which incensed him further.

"I never killed anyone who had

already surrendered!" he shouted.
He was short of breath now, but refused the chair that I offered him.
"Well? Had they surrendered?"
I didn't answer, which was all the answer he needed.
"There'll be a reckoning for this, Heracles" he whispered, hoarsely.
"Is this going to be a long lecture?" I asked.
He shook his head.
"You've brought shame and dishonour on yourself and your family"
He was very short of breath now.
"This family.. is... you've contaminated us all"
I'd had enough. I made my excuses and said I had somewhere I needed to be.
But he hadn't finished.
"And you've offended the gods!!"
I informed him that if -if- the gods existed, I really didn't give a toss if I'd offended them.
He reeled in shock. For a moment, I thought he was about to have some kind of seizure.
But then he turned and set off

towards the gates.

Good riddance, I thought, I didn't need his approval.

I called after him. "Take care, old man!"

Yes, I know, dismally adolescent. As I watched him trudging away up the path, I waited to see if he'd look back at me.

But he didn't turn, he just kept on going.

Fine. It didn't matter. He wasn't even my real father. His opinion wasn't important.

I sat down and resumed my breakfast.

That evening I got drunk. Very drunk. Alone.

When I woke up the next morning, the entire house had been wrecked.

I just nipped downstairs for a drink (of water). I'd developed a raging thirst, almost as if I could feel the dust of Thebes in my throat. I didn't realize how long I'd been writing.

As I guzzled down several glasses of Adam's ale (as your Dad used to call it) I spent a few moments looking out of the kitchen window.

The moonlight was flickering across the Firth and picking out a ghostly squad of seagulls as they bobbed on the water.

It felt very calming.

I've lived in thousands of places and I've never felt as comfortable as I have here.

Mostly, of course, that is down to you. This is, I think, the longest I've stayed anywhere. You made a piece of tumbleweed put down some roots, Bessie.

But it's this place, too, that has cast some kind of spell over me. The light is magical here; it offers you something new every day. With its canvass of huge skies, shimmering water and endless beaches, it somehow never repeats itself.

I would have loved to just carry on gazing out of that window, as I have done on so many occasions. But I know that I must crack on.

As I entered my early twenties, fame started to turn sour. Experiences were beginning to replicate and the thrill-seeking became empty and contrived.

Perhaps I was starting to grow up. The Queen, in particular, developed into a repetitive and especially absurd problem.

It's very hard *not* to get the giggles when you're having sex with a woman who's dressed as Medusa and is wearing a wig that incorporates live snakes. (Her idea, so it's her own fault she got bitten)

The public also became a very irksome problem.

Everywhere I went I had to wade through crowds. Some ~~just~~ people just wanted a handshake, others wanted endorsements, or simply to touch my tunic, which was rumoured to have magical healing properties.

One woman would, physically, try to cling on to me wherever I went. She was like a limpet.

I tried to deal with her in a

humane and civilised way. But she was relentless.

So, in the end, I had a word with the King who marooned her on an island.

There were many other irritants. For instance, in Itoni, an extremely large man started passing himself as me.

He slept with dozens of women and managed to procure various free goods and services on the basis that he was the legendary Heracles.

He didn't have a lion-coat, but apparently he just told people that it was in the wash.

Eventually, this chancer was rumbled and put on trial. My slippery lawyer, Xylopraxes, was hired to defend him. Xylopraxes argued that these were victimless crimes. The women who'd slept with this fake Heracles had enjoyed the cheap thrill and the men who'd given or lent him cash had, similarly, had a few moments of feeling special.

It was a resourceful defence and it might have worked if the jury had not included five men whose wives had been serviced by the gigantic pretender.

So the man was garotted in front of a large, enthusiastic crowd.

(I know this sounds grim, Bessie, but for thousands of years this sort of thing was mankind's idea of justice. Still is – in some places)

I didn't witness any of this myself, the whole story was related to me by Xylopraxes.

"The problem is" he explained "there are dozens of these fakes out there. They're like locusts, devouring your good name."

I should have stopped listening there and then, but there was something hypnotic about him once he got going.

"Y'see, my lad, out in these fly-infested backwaters, they have no idea what the *real* Heracles looks like."

Where was he going with this?

"They've never clapped eyes on your true magnificence."

I told Xylopraxes that I had

no intention of going on tour.

"No, no, no, but if, say, accurate depictions of you were widely available then..."

I asked him to be more specific.

"Well, you know, if there were pictures of you on wall-hangings, or garments, or bed-linen, then..."

The idea of my face being widely available seemed pretty vulgar, as did making money out of it. But Xylopraxes waved his chubby, bejewelled hands around and claimed that I'd misunderstood his suggestion.

"This isn't for commercial gain, my boy," he said "no, no, no, it is purely to curtail the activities of all these shameless charlatans."

I still wasn't convinced. My image on bed-linen? What would that look like?

"Ah! Now!" he explained, pointing a podgy finger at me "By a stroke of luck, I happen to have some with me."

Well, you can guess the outcome. He was someone who wouldn't take 'no' for an answer and, in the end, you say yes just to shut them up.

Within a matter of weeks, I could not go anywhere without seeing my own face staring back at me.

At a palace banquet, as I finished my meal, my face slowly appeared at the bottom of the dish.

In the municipal baths, I watched hairy-arsed men wiping themselves dry with my face.

I was everywhere, haunting myself.

One morning, I challenged Xylopraxes.

"Why's this stuff being sold here in Thebes?" I demanded. "Thebans know what I look like."

Xylopraxes said he'd close his shops in Thebes if that's what I wanted.

"I'm sure the charities will all understand."

I hadn't heard him mention charities before.

"Oh yes, any Heracles-related goods sold in Theban outlets, the money goes to charities. After running costs have been deducted, obviously. And distribution costs. And marketing, postage, administration, overheads, sundries and so forth and so on"

To answer your question, my love,

yes, I did fall for that as well.

To be more accurate, I couldn't be bothered to question it. I couldn't be bothered to do anything because, by this time, I had slid into quite a deep depression.

My only escape from these feelings of imprisonment was to go fishing.

You came fishing with me once, do you remember? You called it 'staring at liquid wallpaper'. But that's what I quite like about it – the way it can empty your brain.

And it's not always dull, *the* most defining experience of my life happened while I was fishing, when I was at my lowest.

Near my house was a wee, hidden loch. My secret place.

I'd sit and listen to the rustle of the reeds and the hum of the insects, waiting for the float to dip.

It didn't matter if the float never dipped. I wasn't really there to catch anything, just to try to stop the hell of thinking –

– to simply not exist.

On the fateful morning, I was angling with a rod I'd made from the branch of a birch tree.

A heron was patrolling the shallows. Every few minutes, I'd glimpse a flash of blue, as a kingfisher arrowed into the water.

A heat-haze was shimmering above the lake and I'd drunk a flask of elder wine, so my eyelids were growing heavy when, with a c-rack, the rod bowed till the tip almost touched the water.

I jumped to my feet and caught the briefest, heart-stopping glimpse of a huge rainbow of a fish, bulleting through the reeds with my hook in its mouth!

Instinctively, I tightened my grip on the rod, but with a loud snap, the rod broke in half and the top half started travelling at speed across the surface of the lake, before suddenly being dragged beneath the water.

As the ripples lapped gently against the silence, I stood open-mouthed in shock.

What a fish!

I had never seen one of such size, beauty and power.

The water was still now. Everything was still. Strangely still.

The heron stood frozen, like a garden ornament.

The dragonflies rested, motionless, on completely static rushes. No butterflies took to the air. No gnats flew in giddy patterns. The buzz of insects had fallen silent.

It was as if there had been a power-cut.

I felt the hairs on the back of my neck start to rise.

What was happening? There was not a single, tiny leaf that was daring to move.

It felt like Time had stopped.

Then I saw it! The same extraordinary fish, hurtling through the reeds, left to right – a blur of shining energy.

And now it had jackknifed and it was accelerating towards me, that's how it seemed. It kept picking up speed as it zipped towards me, straight at me, so fast, until, a few feet away from me, it leapt high out of the water, gave one lazy flick of its tail and climbed still higher!

Now it was framed against the sky, several feet above my head; jewels of water falling from its skin and every scale a different, dazzling colour!

I whooped with joy. Exhilaration was coursing through my body and every inch of me was ~~sensitised~~ sensitised and tingling. I knew that I was witnessing a wonder that was extraordinary and unique.

And yet, still, this fish was climbing as it soared way, way above my head!

Then, as it started to lose momentum, this perfect, perfect fish curved its back into an arc and, as it hung, majestically in mid-air, it looked down at me and yelled "Surprise!!!"

Well, it was a shock — of course it was — to be shouted at by a fish.

But my immediate reaction

was laughter. Nervous laughter, perhaps, but loud and elated.

Then I stopped dead in mid-laugh.

My wonderful fish had turned into a man – a tall, handsome, bearded, laughing man!

There'd been no perceptible moment of transformation, just like in a dream, when you realise that the ticket-collector you were talking to is now your mother.

The ex-fish was still hanging in mid-air. He had golden-brown skin, blonde curls and blue eyes that glittered as if there were fairy lights behind the pupils.

"You should see your face!" he laughed. "That's one of the funniest startled faces I've ever seen and I've seen hundreds."

He floated through the air towards me and set himself down on the ground a few feet away.

It felt like every hair on my body had stood to attention.

For the first time in many

years, I felt scared.

"Don't be frightened" he said. "I'm family. Did you like the fish?"

I mumbled that, yes, I had liked the fish.

"Good, good. You know who I am, of course."

I've no idea why I hesitated. For some reason, in my mind's eye, I had always imagined that a God would be taller.

He was six foot, but he was shorter than me. I'd not yet fully understood that he could be whatever size he chose. I was a wee bit slow on the uptake back then, as you'll have noticed.

My hesitation did not go down well.

"Come on, Muscles, wakey-wakey, what's the matter? Forgotten to put your brain in this morning? How many clues do you need?"

Casually, he threw a bolt of lightning from his fingertips.

I stammered, bowing my head, that he was mighty Zeus, king of gods.

"The boy's a genius!" he chuckled. "Now, I can't stop long, so listen hard, Heracles" He paused and shook his head. "'Heracles'..ridiculous name. What were your parents thinking of?"

I explained that they'd wanted to protect me from the wrath of Hera.

Zeus burst out laughing and shook birds out of the trees and reeds.

"Oh dear... mortals" he sighed, shaking his head again "Bless 'em"

I asked if my parents fears had been misplaced.

He cocked his head to one side and studied me.

"I don't answer questions. One of the perks. Now then, Her-a-cles.."

He pulled a childish face as he stretched my name.

"Usually, I let people make their own mistakes, but you've been making a lot of them recently so because of our... 'special connection' I've come to advise you that you must try harder to be less of an idiot. Got that? It's not hard. Use your brain to avoid mistakes, that's my tip, because all of the ill-considered choices you make, you will have to live with for an unimaginably l-o-n-g time"

I was struggling to take all this in. It felt as if too many thoughts and emotions were trying to crowd through the same gap.

Zeus seemed exasperated by my confusion.

"You will not die as mortals do" he explained, slow and loud, as if I was a foreigner.

By now, I'd formed a definite dislike of Zeus. You don't expect a God to constantly stoop to sarcasm, do you.

(You would absolutely hate him, my love. He's a smartarse – and 100% patriarch)

I tried my hardest to pin him down. I asked if he was telling me that I would live forever. But he just looked at me with a crooked smile.

"Do you want to hear a joke?"

I must have looked thrown, because he started giggling.

"Why the face, muscles? Why wouldn't a God like jokes? That's stupid. I'm the God of Everything and jokes definitely come under the extremely general heading of Everything. Life's a comedy. You won't get through it without jokes."

He then told me a puerile joke about a man who walks into a restaurant and orders a dog--shit salad.

The restaurant is thrown, but he doesn't want to lose the custom. So he gets his dog to shit into some salad and then serves it, rather apprehensively, to the customer.

No sooner has the customer started eating the salad, than he exclaims "Oh, eurgh! That is, oh, totally disgusting!"

The panicking restauranteur races over and asks him what the problem is - and the customer says "There's a man over there and he's picking his nose!"

Exactly. I didn't laugh either. But Zeus was folded in half.

"You don't get it, do you, Muscles? It's about egocentricity. None of you are self-aware."

He copied my blank face.

"Duh! You all think that what other people do is disgusting. You all - oh never mind, I give up"

He shook his head in disdain.

His showboating was really starting to grate on my nerves, so I decided to challenge him.

"You said I'd made mistakes, what mistakes?"

"Steady, tiger, I ask the questions"

"Oh just give a straight answer for once!" I snapped.

Suddenly, the air felt itchy and my whole body began to tingle.

"That's no way to talk to your father" he said, in a low, steady tone. He moved closer and a wave of heat hit me, like someone had opened the door of an enormous oven.

"But then, you have a history of being a disrespectful son, don't you"

I went to answer, but found that I was, physically, unable to speak.

"If you persist in offending against the laws of Nature, then your punishment will follow."

Still, I was incapable of any sound.

"So think on, boy, before you repeat the profanity of that massacre at the Crone's Mouth. Think on, before your all-consuming pride makes you address Amphitryon as if he was a rag-arsed nobody. Think on."

He waved a hand and gave me back my voice.

"Hypocrite!" I yelled. "You have the sheer, unmitigated gall to talk of respecting Amphitryon! You impersonated him to seduce my mother!"

Zeus began to laugh nostalgically. "Yes, yes I did. What a night that was."

My blood was boiling with righteous anger, there'd be no holding back now.

"What is wrong with you? You're some kind of defective, always.. hopping into these stupid guises!"

"You liked the fish."

"Wha.. what you did to my mother was just.. just polite rape! I'll take no lectures from you. One minute you're a swan, the next you're a bull, you belong in a circus!"

He told me to stop and think, but I crashed on.

"And what's it all *for*, eh? Eh? Answer me that. All you do is inflict cruelty on people.. I..I don't understand it."

Zeus put on a new voice – the kind you use when talking to a baby.

"Does Diddums want a god he can understand? Does he? Yes he does, yes, he—"

I interrupted God. "I want one I can respect. You're no better than us. No, no worse. Because of all the harm you do. Well, I.. I refuse to accept your authority."

Zeus slowly quoted my words back at me, weighing each one.

"You.. refuse.. to.. accept.. my.."

"You heard me!"

He smiled, or rather his mouth smiled, not his eyes.

"You'll have plenty of time to accept my authority," he said, calmly. "Plenty of time, little Heracles."

Then he was seized by laughter again, bent double, his shoulders heaving.

"What's so funny?" I snapped.

"Well..." he dabbed his eyes, "I came here to urge you to stop making so many mistakes.. and you've just made the biggest one of your life."

I'd be lying if I said I wasn't scared, Bessie, but I was damned if I was going to show it.

So I told God to go fuck himself.

A mistake. With hindsight.

Zeus fixed me with brightly shining eyes.

"Whoops. You've gone way too far, little Heracles. There'll be *full* punishment"

"Punish me now then" I cried.

"No. Not now" he said "You're not happy enough".

And with that he was gone, vanished into the water.

That's how it happened, Bess.

I remember every moment, every word, as if it was yesterday. I lost control. I chose the wrong words. I was so angry with everyone.

After Zeus had done his disappearing trick, the sounds of birdsong and the humming of the insects resumed. Then, slowly, one by one, dead fish began to float to the surface.

He had poisoned my lake.

So there you have it; an eye-witness description of God. God in person, not a voice in a cave, or a burning bush.

He looked a wee bit like old Donald Laidlaw - a younger version. I'd try and draw God for you but you know that I'm rubbish at drawing.

Actually, not being able to draw is something that I find extremely reassuring, because the simple fact that there are things I can't do is a confirmation that — whatever I am — I am definitely not a God.

I may be destined to live forever, (possibly, Zeus's words on that subject were a little cryptic) but, clearly, if I were a God I would be able to draw brilliantly.

A God would also be brilliant at Scrabble, multi-tasking, ~~and~~ smalltalk and all the other things I'm useless at. (You've probably got your own list, Bessie)

A God, by definition, can do absolutely anything. A God knows everything, even the future. A God never needs to learn, discover or grow.

What could be more boring? Imagine living a life devoid of all doubt or curiosity because you've already decided the outcome.

I may be some freakish hybrid but I'm glad that I'm not 100% divine. Give me people over gods any day. I[illegible]perfection makes people better co[illegible]pany.

The trouble with human-beings is that they die.
There's no way round that. Sometimes you have to watch them fade from view and sometimes they are snatched away.

That's why I try not to get too attached to them. The certainty that I will lose them and have to see them grow old – perhaps even into ghosts of themselves – is painful.

But you got through my defences, Bess.

That's not to say I've never formed any relationships. From time to time, life has thrown me a friend.

When I was about 200 years old, I rescued a man from some Scythian hill-farmers who were about to kill him because he had red hair.

In many ancient cultures (especially out in the sticks) red hair was viewed with suspicion.

In my experience, there's always something that can get someone killed. People are forever looking for something to fear. It's a human need.
The fellow I saved was called Nestas.

He was a man of great wit and warmth. We were travelling companions for about ten years, but then he picked up an infection and that was that.

I was friends with Oddyseus, of course, for a while. And there was an early Christian, called Eland, who I spent a lot of time with.

He was thoughtful and interesting but, like many of the early Christians, he gradually became more and more paranoid.

St. Paul (or Paul, as he was then) liked to keep his followers in a state of febrile watchfulness. Any rival sects, or outsiders, were nearly always 'puppets of Satan'.

You would not have liked Paul. He had a real problem with women.

In the end, ~~was~~ inevitably, the fact that I didn't appear to age attracted suspicion. People used to age much faster back then, so I stood out more.

When I started hearing dark whispers about magic, I moved on; as I always did whenever that nonsense started.

In the 1500s, in Tuscany, I befriended an inventor and polymath named Fachetti.

You won't find him in the history books – though he deserves to be included – because he wouldn't cave in to the demands of his rich patrons. He was one of those men who refused to be owned.

I lodged with Fachetti for seven years. Sometimes I helped him with his work, especially if it needed some muscle.

On more than one occasion, I had to drag his latest flying-machine out of a bog. He was an indefatigable experimenter.

Eventually, he was burnt as a heretic and I was not there to save him.

I've always felt that I let him down. I still miss the wide-ranging conversations that we used to have late into the night.

I felt comfortable with him. But I never trusted him with my secret, Bess. You're the only one I've ever trusted that much.

There were no women, if that's

what you're wondering.

After what happened in Thebes, I completely shut down that part of my psyche. I suppose that felt safest.

I did have some platonic friendships. There was a widow in Avignon called Monique. I'd got to know her husband, Bertrand, who was an aide-de-camp for Napoleon.

Bertrand was mortally wounded at Austerlitz, but he asked me to deliver some personal mementoes to his wife.

So I kept that promise. And I lived close by for several years, and I helped her as she built up a small business making wedding dresses.

I liked her a lot. She was funny and honest; it was like having a sister.

But she suddenly grew old and started to confuse me with her dead father. Then the day came when she didn't recognise me at all and I knew I could be no further help to her.

Not the classic image of Heracles, is it? Helping out in a dress shop. Hardly the stuff of epic poems.

There is a chapter in the legend of Heracles that has always left me feeling wistful.

According to the myth, I once challenged Death to a wrestling match in order to save the life of a dying friend.

Needless to say, I won. Death accepted defeat very graciously, and my friend was spared.

If it were possible, I would have been happy - and honoured - to have wrestled with Death to save Nestas, Eland, Fachretti or Monique.

I would fight Death for you. I'd fight with unwavering and relentless ferocity.

But you cannot wrestle with Death any more than you can wrestle with water or air.

Because Death is not a character, nor an enemy. It's a process. It's something that happens. There's no contesting or bargaining, you just have to accept that the older you get the more your life will fill with ghosts.

It is conceivable, I suppose, that some of the friends I lost were taken from me by Zeus.

He likes to keep me guessing, that's all part of the game.

So perhaps he engineered the burning of Fachetti and addled the mind of Monique.

I certainly wouldn't put it past him.

As I write, a crow has landed on the window-sill. It's unusual to see a crow out and about after dark.

The bird's head is cocked to one side and it seems to be studying me. That's one of his mannerisms.

It could be Him. Again, just letting me know he's around.

Though he doesn't normally take on the guise of something as mundane as a crow.

He prefers large, glossy mammals — usually with absurdly long penises.

No. It's just a crow. He's got me jumping at shadows.

Also, that crow is about 8 feet away and if Zeus were that close every single hair on my body would be standing on end.

There were only a few friendships like the ones I've described, and that's spread across thousands of years, so my average is pretty low.

In all that time, across all those centuries, I have only fallen in love twice.

Here, with you. And in Thebes.

So this is it. The part I've been dreading. The part about Megara and the family we started.

Hell, this is going to be hard. It's going to involve releasing memories that I've kept locked away for so long.

But it has to be told.

Even if I can make no sense of it.

And it will be so very hard for you to read it.

If I owe you complete honesty – and after all the deceptions I definitely think I do – then I'm afraid that neither of us can be spared. So here comes the most nightmarish part of my story.

More nightmarish than all the

murders and the massacres? I'm afraid so.

But I'll begin with the happy bit. As I've mentioned, Megara didn't seem very impressed with me at first, (and that's putting it mildly)

For my part, I disliked her intensely, though I thought about her all the time. As soon as I saw her gliding towards me, I would feel clumsy and oafish.

But all that changed in a single evening, one moonlit evening—just like in a song.

It was a few months after my encounter with the talking fish. The experience had left me feeling that nothing really mattered or made any sense.

I'd descended into a mental state that was a mix of every negative emotion. There's no word to describe it. Even in German, It would need an impossibly long compound noun.

When people spoke to me I went through the motions of answering them but, for the most part, the conversations whirred around my ears like mosquitoes.

The moonlit evening in question was the backdrop to the Queen's birthday party. Apparently, she was thirty-six.

Initially, I had declined the invitation and stayed at home. But then my mother had paid an unexpected visit. I couldn't face being harangued so I used the party as an excuse to get away from her.

Not very filial, I know, but I needed to get out of there before the wailing started. (Believe me, she made your Mum look like a ray of sunshine)

As soon as I arrived at the palace, the Queen dragged me into a cupboard where, despite a lot of effort on her part, I was unable to rise to the occasion.

She was not happy. I told her that it was no reflection on her because recently I'd had no libido (which was true.)

But every excuse I made just seemed to enrage her more.

In the end, she slapped my face and stormed off, shouting over her

shoulder "Some fucking demi-god you are!" (loose translation)
Most of the guests would have heard her, including the King, but I was past caring.
I just wanted to hide.
Sadly, Xylopraxes found me.
He wanted to talk me through his plans for a luxury resort, where rich folk could pay through the nose to play skittles with the legendary Heracles.
I managed to give that fat shark the slip, but then I got cornered by some unctious toadie who wondered if I'd ever thought of investing in stadium construction.
Eventually, I climbed over a wall at the back of the royal gardens and sat quietly on the riverbank, watching the moonlight as it snaked and shimmered across the black water.
The moon was full, just as it is tonight. The Firth is silvery smooth, like silk.
Behind the hills, there's a faint suggestion of pink in the night sky. You're a lucky woman to have

this wonderful place as your home.

The party was so rowdy that I presumed no-one had noticed me slip away. But, to my surprise, Megara appeared, tall and slender, in a dark blue gown.

"Are you hiding?" she asked, picking up a stone and throwing it in the river.

I told her that I couldn't face being sociable.

"Oh I know that feeling" she said. "My mother's very angry with you."

I mumbled that I didn't care.

She threw another stone.

"You're very subdued tonight"

"Sorry" I muttered.

"Don't be sorry. I like it"

Then she offered me a pebble.

"Go on, throw it. Might make you feel better"

I skimmed the pebble across the surface of the water, very nearly hitting a swan.

For about twenty minutes, we just stood, side by side, skimming stones. The silence didn't feel awkward, so neither of us tried to fill it. I was struck by how comfortable and natural it seemed.

Then, from nowhere, she said "Just in case you're thinking of taking a lunge at me... don't."

"I don't lunge" I informed her.

"Only because you never have to" she laughed.

I'd heard her laugh at me many times before, but this was the first time that the laughter had felt playful rather than mocking.

"Well you're perfectly safe with me, Heracles. I don't lunge either. I won't be dragging you off into a cupboard."

It should have been embarassing that she knew so much about my sexual history, but somehow it wasn't.

It was relaxing to be in a situation where so little needed to be said. I noticed that, for the first time in months, I didn't have a headache.

I threw another stone into the night and there was an ominous thump.

"I think you just put a hole in the royal barge" she whispered.

"Sorry"

"I've never liked it." She handed me a new stone. "See if you can sink it"

So that was our first romantic evening, Boss, standing beneath the moonlight trying to sink her Dad's boat.

You and I had to make do with dinner at Nando's, didn't we.

That conversation was the first one where Megara didn't try to take lumps out of me.

Over the days that followed, the conversations became more frequent and more and more relaxed. This woman was different, I began to realize.

I promise I won't write too much about my love for another woman. I know that could be galling. I'll keep it to the minimum that's necessary.

I can hear your car pulling in, so I'd bett

30th November

My god, Bessie, what a night! My mind's still racing and I'm not sure where to begin. I'm so sorry. This is all my fault.

It's four-thirty in the morning and I've just got back from the hospital.

The doctors are saying it's too early to make any predictions. You're in a coma. They won't be able to make any proper assessment until the swelling around your brain starts to reduce.

That's what they said.

But one doctor — a young fella who looked as if he hadn't slept for weeks — told me that they've seen many patients with head injuries like yours and that, in a significant percentage of cases, they made a full recovery.

I wish I'd asked what a 'significant percentage' was. Or perhaps it's better not to know the odds. It's not like I can affect them now.

I failed to protect you, that's the bottom line.

I'*m* the reason you're unconscious in that Intensive Care Unit. I should have had the guts to just leave, as soon as you told me about Billy and the White Stag.

I should have guessed that He would pull a stunt like this.

The doctors said that it would be good for you to hear familiar voices, that it might help because they don't know whether patients in comas are, in fact, conscious at some deep, dream-like level.

So I sat by your bed and talked. For about four hours.

It wasn't easy. You looked so frail and battered. The burns, they say, will not be a long-term problem. Although, it's not easy to believe that, because they look pretty serious right now.

I feel a little lost without you and your infallible bullshit detector. Doctors are hard to read.

I didn't know what to talk about at first. I found myself, ludicrously, attempting to make smalltalk with someone incapable of responding. You'd have laughed. (Perhaps you were laughing)

In the end, I just babbled like an idiot. Not like taciturn Malcolm, more like a teenager who'd taken a few wee pills.

I tried calling up happy memories; like that rooftop terrace at your Uncle's place where the swifts swooped and spun around our ears, almost deafening us with all that wonderful, joyous screeching.

Your face was illuminated with exhilaration. I'll never forget that.

And I burbled nervously about the holidays we'd had and all the memorable experiences we'd shared — anything to drown out the beeping of the machines.

I did some funny memories as well. Like when your mother got drunk and we found her buried in that childrens' ball-pond.

Or the time we were having sex in the woods and those Boy Scouts stumbled across us and you told them we were botanists who'd had to take off all our clothes because they were full of ants.

You lied with such confidence that I found it a little scary.

I also told you that I loved you. Just in case that counted for something.

In the end, I ran out of things to say. So I just sat there like a lemon (as you would say) and contemplated my utter helplessness.

It's a horrible dilemma. Logic dictates that I should leave immediately so that there's no further risk of Zeus hunting you.

On the other hand, I can't *imagine* leaving you when you're in this condition. I *have* to know that you're going to be alright. I've no idea what to do for the best.

I feel paralysed, like a rabbit in the headlights.

I would happily have sat at your bedside all night, just holding your hand and listening to you breathe, but your brother arrived so I stepped out.

My plan had been to simply hang around the hospital, ~~But~~ But the doctors kept asking if they could run more tests on me, so

I slipped away and came home.

As I left, Billy Ballantyne's father was in the reception area, effing and blinding at all the staff and informing two doctors that they were wankers.

At one point, he started gesticulating, angrily, with one of his crutches and fell crashing to the floor.

One of the nurses giggled and he threatened to sue her.

My understanding is that Billy is in a very similar condition to you – 'too early to say'.

When I got home I tried lying down for a while, but there's absolutely no chance of me sleeping, so I might as well keep writing this, in the hope that some day soon you will be well enough to read it.

Once you've recovered, you'll no doubt hear many versions of last night's events, so here's mine.

The car that I'd heard pulling in was not yours. It was Fraser Laidlaw and, as soon as I heard the panicky tooting of the car-horn, I knew something was horribly wrong.

Perhaps you sense things more quickly when you've been waiting for them to happen.

Fraser drove us at breakneck speed through the back lanes towards the red glow that I'd noticed earlier behind the hills, which was now more intense.

By the time we got to the school, the blaze had taken hold. Flames were leaping out of most of the windows and the roof was already burning fiercely.

Large, glowing cinders were slowly spiralling into the night and the acrid sting of chemicals was making it painful to breathe.

The Emergency Services were there in force – six fire-engines, maybe more – though, to my eyes, nobody seemed to be actually doing anything!

There was a lot of shouting and running and some panicking, but no action!

Amid all this confusion I spotted the Deputy Head, wrapped in silver foil and being led towards an ambulance by paramedics.

He was clearly in shock but I had no time for niceties, so I grabbed him by the shoulders and demanded to know where you were.

He stammered that he hadn't seen you come out, but that someone had seen you heading into the gymnasium.

This was terrible news. The gymnasium building was ablaze from one end to the other, and part of the roof had collapsed!

What remained looked like it could disintegrate any second, so I started striding towards the inferno.

There was a sudden whoosh – like a firework – and a small, metal tank was hurled into the sky.

A policeman was moving all the gawpers further back up the road. He called after me, but I ignored him.

There was only one thought in my head, I was coming to find you.

"Sir! Sir!" yelled a fireman "No further, please!"

Then another fireman – more senior – stepped in front of me. He was shouting that the integrity of the building had been compromised but I just ploughed straight through him. I'm sorry if he got hurt. I didn't mean to send him flying.

A couple of policemen made the mistake of trying to grab me, but they might just as well have stepped in front of a train.

I think I may have heard some fractures.

After all the dust has settled, Bessie, I'd be grateful if you could convey my sincere apologies.

When I reached the doors to the gym I discovered that they were locked, or jammed, so I simply tore them from their hinges.

Instantly, flames surged out, hunting for this new supply of oxygen.

So the entrance now looked totally impassable – it was a wall of fire!

To be honest, I can't really recall what happened next.

But I suppose I must have walked straight through the flames.

I can remember the intense heat inside the building. (I've

got a pair of badly scorched eyebrows now – not a great look)

I can remember the hissing and the roaring of the flames, and the crack and the pop of bubbling metal and disintegrating wood.

But most of all, I remember the fear.

I couldn't see you!

I couldn't see anything but black, billowing smoke.

I dropped to my knees and began crawling around in the low corridor of air beneath the toxic, curling cloud.

I suppose I must have been finding it difficult to breathe but, again, I have no memory of that.

I have absolutely no sense of how long I was searching for you. It felt like an eternity.

You know that expression 'to have your heart in your mouth'? That is literally how it felt as the blind panic engulfed me. There's no better description.

When, at last, I found you, I I was scared that I might be hallucinating. Your lovely hair was

thickly-matted with blood and the roof-beam that had done the damage was burning next to you. Blood was trickling out of your ear. The blood looked dark.
You seemed to be alive, but I couldn't be sure.

The next thing I knew I was walking towards the fleet of ambulances with you cradled in my arms.

I remember some cheering, but most of the faces I could see through the smoke were wide-eyed with astonishment.

Fraser Laidlaw came rushing towards us.

"Jesus H. Christ, Malcolm, how the fuck did you manage that? Are you made from fucking titanium or something?"

Very carefully, we loaded you into an ambulance, with the paramedics keeping your head as still as possible.

Mrs. Henderson scuttled across the grass, her face blackened with soot.

"Is Bess OK?" she shouted.

A medic told her you were alive, as he closed the doors of the ambulance.

Then a police officer started firing questions at her. Was everyone accounted for? Had she done a tally?

"We can't find Billy Ballantyne" she shouted over the wailing of a siren. "One of the kids saw him run into the Language Lab."

I saw Fraser Laidlaw's face turn white. He was looking at the Language Lab as it was being swallowed by the fire.

"He's got no chance, poor kid"

A few yards away stood a group of firemen in special suits, kitted out with breathing equipment.

They looked poised, eager to enter the inferno, but an officer was gesturing for them to stand by.

"Just waiting on the assesment, lads!" he shouted.

Flames were licking out of every window of the Language Lab. It looked like the assessment would arrive too late for Billy.

So I went in and got him.
Everyone will mistake my actions for heroism, but no bravery was required because I knew that the fire could not kill me.

There's one last detail that's worth the telling.

After I had rescued Billy, as the emergency vehicles busied backwards and forwards – just before the main building collapsed in slow motion – I noticed a dim glow at the edge of the woods.

Peering through the smoke and flashing lights, I could just discern the outline of a large, white stag.

He was watching it all, Bess. And he wanted me to know he was watching.

Well, I was pumped, really buzzing, and I wasn't going to be intimidated.

So if, when you're better, you hear accounts of how Malcolm went berserk and started shouting obscenities at trees, that's the explanation.

He was taunting me. That's why

I was yelling "Who the fuck have you come as? Bambi's Dad? Fuck off back to Olympus, you infantile prick!" (And other such gems)

It was reckless, but I was too distraught and angry to care.

Your brother just texted me. Your condition is unchanged and your medical team are having a meeting at 8.30 in the morning. So I'll be back at the hospital for that.

I'm finding all this a wee bit tricky, Bess.

I'm doing my best to remain calm. Unlike most men, I can't have a drink to steady my nerves. And I have no god to pray to — just to run from.

I'm ending a lot of sentences with prepositions, aren't I. You're always telling the kids not to do that. Well, I'm up against even more time pressure – and general pressure — so I'm afraid that style is now <u>def</u>initely a luxury that I don't have room for. (Sorry)

You're always telling me not

to fret over things I can't control.

But it's so hard to accept that you're trapped in your secret underworld while I'm left powerless. Orpheus had it easy. At least he could do something.

That story, of course, is more invented, childish nonsense. But I have a true story that needs finishing. And it will give me something to think about that is not the image of you connected to all those machines.

The first few weeks of my relationship with Megara consisted of natural conversations and equally natural silences.

Each morning I woke up excited about the day ahead – a feeling that I'd nearly forgotten.

But, though I was excited I was also apprehensive. What was the depth of Megara's feelings? How did she see me? Wouldn't I always be the arrogant fuckwit who used to shag her mother?

I put that to her once. She just smiled and said "Nobody's perfect" (In many ways, she was quite like you)

Don't worry, I don't intend to make any observations about love. I'm hardly an expert.

I've only fallen in love twice, though those two experiences had very different shapes.

With Megara, there was no one, single, moment when I realized I had fallen in love. It happened in increments.

With you, though, it was different. I thought I'd surrounded myself with impenetrable walls of indifference. And yet—and I've only recently come to understand this—I was hooked on you from the moment I saw you hurling obscenities at that poor man in the fluorescent tabard.

No doubt you'd claim that what I'm describing is lust; but I know better.

Alright, yes, there may have been an element of lust. A small element. Let's split the difference and call what I was feeling 'lovst'.

Not a word? Well it is now.

The initial progress of my romance with Megara was decidedly cautious.

Don't forget, this was all completely new to me.

I'd not had an emotional connection with a woman before.

The courtship process was especially unsettling because I'd never had to court. All I'd known thus far was bored, unhappy women throwing themselves at me.

In sexual terms, I was a veteran, But, emotionally, I was still a novice.

There was a wariness in Megara as well. She'd been damaged by the pressures of her upbringing.

Like a lot of Princesses, she'd had to live under constant scrutiny. When you're a Princess, whatever you do, everyone feels entitled to have an opinion about it.

Megara had developed a reflex defence. As soon as she felt any kind of pressure, she would push back against it.

And there was constant pressure from her father, the King, who was disconcertingly keen for us to get married.

Instinctively, Megara never wanted

to please her father, for the simple reason that she hated him.

He was a lecher, a bully, a crook and a tyrant. Whenever she talked about him she invariably called him a 'zyraki'— which was a Theban slang term for the rectum.

So, although we loved each other's company and felt totally at ease together, the way ahead seemed uncertain and a wee bit frightening.

One morning, as we sat by an artificial brook in the palace gardens, (Everything in those gardens was artificial) I summoned up the courage to raise the topic of our future.

I began by telling Megara that I was scared and didn't know what to do.

She looked into my eyes as if she was reading a book.

"What is it that scares you?" she asked.

I hesitated. "Well, um.. lots of things are scaring me.. including you"

She laughed at the notion, so I tried to find the words to explain.

"The thing is... well.. you always gave off such a... you always made me feel that... in your eyes.. I didn't measure up to much.. that I was shallow and.."

"Oh that was *then*" she protested.

"Yes I know, but.. what if you were right?"

She reached out and held my hand.

"I wasn't right."

I blurted out my big problem.

"I don't have any idea how.. to set about wooing you".

She smiled at the quaintness of the term.

"Wooing me?"

"Yes. how do I do that, Megara? How do I woo you?"

She stared into the water for a while. A pelican approached, hoping we might feed it. I clapped my hands to shoo it away.

Eventually, Megara looked up at me and smiled.

"Impress me" she said.

"How?" I asked.

"Nothing to do with running,

or jumping, or throwing stuff. And nothing military. No army-slaying. No, do something meaningful, that doesn't come too easily, that requires time and patience."

She moved a little closer and her gaze intensified.

"Something.. of substance. That'll benefit others. Something that will last"

It was quite a list.

I wanted to be sure that I had understood her.

"You'd like me to do something.. of substance for you?"

"No, Heracles" she grinned. "I'd like you to do something of substance for you"

She could see the hole in me. She'd read me perfectly. She'd understood all the feelings that had been bewildering me.

That's a gift, isn't it, Bessie? Some lucky people - yourself included - can interpret the fragility in people.

That night, as I lay on my roof staring at the stars, I felt a crackle of exhilaration. I would do something impressive.

A few moments ago, I went downstairs to get a glass of water and switched on the news.

We were the second item. The police are saying that the fire was started deliberately.

The usual blame game has begun. Councillor McKenzie was on (surprise, surprise) demanding to know why the emergency services were so slow to respond and why the school caught fire so quickly.

Well, he *is* up for re-election. He praised the quick-thinking of a passer-by (I presume he meant me) but, luckily, the interviewer didn't follow up on that. The last thing I need now is attention.

At the hospital, the doctors had been both bewildered and fascinated by the apparently superficial nature of my injuries.

They'd wanted to subject me to further examinations, but I didn't want to waste time having pointless scans.

Besides, I wanted them to concentrate on the people who'd been genuinely hurt. So I refused any further treatment.

The burns are already healing.

Dawn must be close; because I can hear the oyster-catchers starting to chase each other across the beach and the gulls have started caterwauling on the roof.

Though I've often cursed them, I am going to miss that racket. Perhaps I'll try and find a bolt-hole that is beside the sea.

If I was going to take on some challenge that could be seen as extraordinary, I knew that Thebes was not the place to start.

I could only expect special treatment in Thebes. For me, it would always be Sycophant Gulch. I needed to find a place where I was not a star, less popular, possibly even disliked.

I chose Tiryns. The ruler of that city was my cousin, Eurystheus, and I knew, for a fact, that he absolutely despised me.

The reason for his animosity was always a mystery to me. But he was a very small man and, in my experience, small men like to nurse their hatreds.

I imagine my size brings out

the worst in them.

When you consider all the destruction in human history, it's interesting how much of it has been caused by small, resentful men.

Attila the Hun, for instance, was tiny — and I mean tiny, tiny. So were most of his horde.

In fact, I once came across Attila and his men dancing around their campfires and, for a moment, I thought it was a children's party.

Until I saw the severed heads.

On my arrival in Tiryns, I was escorted to the royal palace, where King Eurystheus greeted me from a throne with a seat that was 8 feet off the ground.

I complimented him on the throne's magnificience. He narrowed his eyes, unsure if I was sending him up.

"It's pure ivory," he said. "I'm sitting on about two hundred elephants' worth of furniture here. Now, how can I help you, my legendary cousin?"

I told him that I was looking for an extraordinary challenge.

"Why here?" he asked, with a hint of suspicion. "Why not Thebes?"

I explained that I was too popular in Thebes.

"Popular?" he grunted, "..right.. so they've forgotten about the murder-thing then?"

"The mob are fickle" I said.

"You don't say. So, you're looking for a challenge that's extraordinary" He sat back in his throne and made popping noises as he weighed the possibilities.

"Erm... you could.. attack Athens"

"Why?"

The King shrugged. "Just a thought" He popped his lips some more.

"It doesn't have to be Athens. Could be Corinth, or-"

I stepped forwards. "The thing is, your-"

"That's close enough"

"..your majesty, I'm not really looking for anything that involves killing. I'd like the task to be, well, meaningful, something lasting and worthwhile.... socially useful"

The King narrowed his eyes once more.

"Are you suggesting my kingdom needs lots of improvements?"

As I said, Bessie, small man, very touchy.

I asked if he could think of anywhere else that might need and welcome my labours.

Eurystheus broke into a sly grin. He called for pen and parchment so that he could write me a letter of introduction to King Augeias, whose kingdom was about ten days walk away.

"I'm sure Augeias will find you something" my cousin said, with a giggly wobble in his voice.

As soon as I'd crossed the border into the kingdom of Augeias, I began to form a very clear impression of its people.

They'd enjoyed about fifty years of affluence, but this had made them fat and complacent.

The citizens I talked to – or

tried to talk to — seemed to have very little interest in the outside world.

They were obsessed with one topic; themselves. Themselves, and their things.

Almost every house had floor mosaics that depicted the owners.

And yet, rich as they clearly were, they seemed to feel that they were being shortchanged. Any conversation quickly became a list of grievances.

For some reason, they were all particularly resentful of the foreign slaves who were doing all the menial jobs.

There was a lot of graffiti that described them as leeches.

Perhaps that's inevitable. Perhaps decades of material comfort always end in bitter dissatisfaction. People get swallowed by their expectations.

Anyway, whatever the reasons were, this nation of spoilt complainers now cared only about their own circumstances.

They didn't care about public life.

They didn't really care about anything. They didn't even care that they were being ruled by a madman.

It took me about two seconds to work out that my cousin had directed me towards a King who was a lunatic.

The crown made from lobster-shells was a clue.

So was the robe made from the skins of several thousand toads. And the very long sceptre, which appeared to be the enbalmed leg of a giraffe.

He was evidently suffering from some fairly advanced stage of dementia.

But he was the King, so no-one was going to put him in a home.

Rather like your great Uncle Bruce, he never used verbs or adjectives.

He just barked nouns at you.

"Stables!" he exploded. "Stink!"

I nodded sympathetically, just as we used to do with your great-Uncle.

"Shit!" yelled Augeias. "Horse-

-shit... cow-shit... goat-shit.. sheep-shit ... Poseidon-shit!"

The old King shook his fists at Poseidon, who was clearly a personal enemy.

"Poseidon...fish-prick!"
He looked to me for confirmation.

"Oh yes, quite..fish-prick" I agreed.
The King roared in approval and then emptied his bowels.

Nothing was said.
Like many insane tyrants, he had an efficient, if permanently nervous, Civil Service.

Its Chief Secretary was called Spirus, and it was he who explained my brief – that I was to clean and rebuild the royal stables.

A contract was drawn up and some fees were agreed, though they were of little importance to me.

Then, Spirus and I rode through verdant countryside for about an hour.

Slowly, insidiously, the air began to fill with a sweet, sickening stench.

I asked Spirus what had gone so badly wrong. Was there nobody managing the stables?

"There used to be," Spirus replied "a capable chap, Dentotes, but the King decided he was an agent for Poseidon. So he threw him to the royal tigers"

He fished in his pocket for a handkerchief.

"His successor was.. well, he upset the King.. in some way, can't recall how exactly.. so he, um.. got.."

"Tigers?"

"Crucified. The King's.. style makes it hard to attract good people. So no-one's managed the stables for 15 years"

He put the handkerchief over his mouth and, as we rounded a bend, we were confronted by a wall of dried-out dung that must have been twelve feet high.

"Some slaves were supposed to clear that" said the muffled voice of the civil servant "but they all ran away... or died."

The scale of the filth was mind-boggling, Bessie. It was nine square miles(ish) of towering excrement that was contaminating and fly-infesting the countryside for

many more miles beyond that.
But I was undaunted.
I hired a team of labourers and – despite the appalling conditions – we managed to clear away the mountain of shit, demolish the rotting stables and replace them with a masterpiece of design and engineering.
When, after many, many months of back-breaking effort (even for me!) I surveyed the finished project I knew I'd achieved something of substance.
It was hailed as a triumph by everyone – apart from the King, whose madness was now so intense that he believed himself to be a badger.
"It's making government very difficult" said Spinus, "the entrance to his den is very narrow. Also, there's a lot of biting."
When he paid me, some of the fee seemed to be missing. Apparently, the shortarse King Eurystheus had taken a cut – a 'finder's fee' as he called it.
I was less than thrilled. So, on my way home, I paid my cousin a surprise visit. His staff said the King was away, on an island, having various top-level meetings. But I found him

hiding in a wine-press.
He paid up. It was the principle.
After over a year's absence, I returned to Thebes.

I came back a very different person to the insecure, lost young man who'd been too scared to woo Megara. I had a new confidence – a confidence that wasn't rooted in the superficial. I threw out the lion-coat. It looked ridiculous to me now.

Megara noticed the change in me immediately. I was more at ease with her and with myself. The mission she'd given me had been successfully completed.

I'd achieved something – *created* something – of genuine substance, something that would stand the test of time.

It was a few months before we heard about the earthquake. Apparently, most of the area had been flattened and my new stables had been swallowed by a crevasse.

It was the work of Zeus, I had no doubt about that.

At first, I was consumed with frustration and rage at having

my achievement so casually erased.
But, to my surprise, those feelings soon dissolved. My new confidence was undamaged. I still had the satisfaction of _knowing_ what I'd achieved.

And I'd discovered the joy of _making_ things. Over many, many centuries now, I've created many things of substance – buildings, artefacts, gardens, bridges – and though He has gone out of his way to destroy most of them, the excitement of creating something new is what has often edged me back from the precipice of insanity.

And yes, that _is_ why I was forever building things in the garden.

Sadly, there won't be time now for me to finish that tree-house. But there's no need to disappoint your nieces. Get Jimmy Kilbride in. He's reliable.

I'm finding it very hard to focus on what I'm writing. I _keep_ picturing you in that hospital bed, connected to all those tubes. I know, 'don't be such a drama queen'

Just now, I had an extremely frightening moment.

There was someone ringing the doorbell, so I put down my pen and went downstairs.

When I opened the door, there was a policeman on the doorstep. It's universal, I suppose, the fear of the policeman at the door. They don't often bring good news, do they.

He was a young lad and he must have seen the dread in my eyes because his first words were "Don't worry. Nothing's happened"

Then he began to tangle his words. "Well - when I - sorry; I meant, y'know, nothing more has happened"

It felt like he'd never had to do anything like this before.

"I'm Police Constable Bremner, I've been asked to do some follow-up. Are you alright, Malcolm?"

I assured him that I was OK, given the circumstances. I asked if this visit was anything to do with the firemen and policemen I'd accidentally injured.

"Not at all, Malcolm" he said.

"You must be in shock. Have you cried?"
I had to stop and think.
I told him that I couldn't really remember.
"Sometimes it helps to have a bit of a cry" P.C. Bremner informed me. "Helps purge the toxins"
I thanked him for the tip.
"There's no rush, Malcolm, but— and this is only when you feel up to it— But Detective Sergeant Greig asks if you could pop into the station at some point. Only he wants to ask you about the threats from Billy Ballantyne. He's been charged. Arson."
I said that I knew Billy had been having mental problems, so, presumably, that would be taken into account.
"We-ll.. there'll be a psychiatric assessment. Are you taking in lots of fluids?
"Yes, thank you, I—
"Do you want the number of the counselling service?"
"No, it's fine. Billy was having hallucinations."
"Doesn't surprise me. Probably off his head. Tragic, isn't it."

We agreed that it was tragic and then he gave me a card covered in helpline numbers.

After he'd left, I sat for a few moments thinking about poor Billy. I felt fairly certain that P.C Bremner must have got his facts wrong. Surely you couldn't charge a person who was in a coma? Also, he was just a boy. A minor.

Gods never seem particularly bothered about a collateral damage, do they. Hundreds of innocent bystanders die in the Bible.

The Almighty wipes out all those Egyptian children just to make the Pharoah submit.

I know, for a fact, that Zeus killed at least thirty thousand people with the earthquake that obliterated my new stables.

It's all crazy. I've been watching this circus for thousands of years and none of it makes any sense.

I'm due back at the hospital soon. Just need to smarten up. If you do come round, I don't want you to see me in a state.

Though there's not much I can do ~~the eyebrows~~. about the eyebrows.

10.45 am.

OK, Bessie, so once again there's good news and bad news.

The good news is that the doctors are sounding a wee bit more optimistic. You're still in a coma, but the swelling around your brain is subsiding fast and they're saying you could surface in the next few days.

So that's all that matters really – that you continue to get better. You're so loved, not just by me. Everyone just wants to see that smile again. And hear that dirty laugh.

The bad news is that I have become a meme.

I suppose I should have guessed that this would happen.

Inevitably, the fire attracted lots of moronic gawpers who wanted to film images of death and disaster on their phones. What many of them got was footage of a huge man, apparently impervious to the smoke and flames, striding into the inferno and then emerging with unconscious figures cradled in his arms.

There are sequences of me rescuing you, and then more close-up sequences of me rescuing Billy. In some of those, you can see that my trousers are on fire.

Apparently, I am all over every corner of the internet and a twitterstorm is raging over how I should be honoured.

I'm on the TV news as well. I'm a 'mystery hero', a 'miracle man' and Sky called me a 'Scottish Superman'. On all the bulletins, they have the same Fire Chief, saying that, in theory, a human-being wouldn't able to breathe in that environment, let alone lift and carry dead weights.

Cheers, pal.

Anyway, Bessie, the upshot is that we currently have half-a-dozen photographers sitting on our front wall. I've had to draw all the curtains.

The voicemails on both my mobile and our landline are almost full with requests for interviews!

How the hell did they get the numbers?

Several of the messages are from a gushy woman who says she's the producer of something called the 'Best of Britain Bravery Awards'.

She says she wants to film a 'segment' about me.

It's a disaster, Bess.

You know what journalists are like. They'll start ferreting around and pretty soon they'll spot how weird I am.

They'll discover that your Malcolm doesn't seem to have any personal history that dates back more than twenty years.

He doesn't seem to have any family. Or health records.

He seems to have sprung from nowhere.

This is not what I need, not on top of everything else.

My passport is a forgery and my national insurance number is a fake. They're bound to work that out.

Wherever I have been, ordinary people have always been curious about me. But, in my long experience, when the press and officialdom start to take an interest, then things can get very unpleasant.

In fact, that's usually when I have to move,

I can hear Piers Morgan leaving a message on the ansaphone!

Perhaps I should agree to appearing on his TV show, then I could kill him as you've often requested.

As I recall, he's top of your "If you really loved me you'd kill them for me" list.

Well, I'm just going to give absolutely no response to any of them and hope that they get bored.

In a few days time, they'll be chasing some other poor sod.

Someone will have tweeted something stupid.

I don't like feeling hunted.

Zeus will be loving every second of this.

This is, arguably, the most difficult corner that he has ever chased me into.

Logically, I should just get the hell out of here. That would be best. For you. For all concerned.

But I need to see you wake up. I need to see you open your eyes. ~~[illegible] next few thousand years [illegible]~~

I can't face the rest of eternity not knowing if you made it back. Though I may have to.

Well, there's no point wasting time with 'ifs', the one concrete thing I can do is complete the labour of finishing this.

Once that's done you'll have the whole story and a full explanation of my disappearance.

Then it will be up to you whether you choose to hate me or not.

So, I returned to Thebes a <u>very</u> changed man.

For perhaps the first time in my life I felt at peace. I wasn't wary, waiting for people to let me down.

The relationship between Megara and I continued to develop.

You'll find this hard to believe, my love, given my track record with the women of Thebes, but my romance with Megara had not yet included sex.

You're probably laughing and shaking your head because.. well, because you know that I'm quite a sexual person. (Now you're definitely laughing)

But it was a question of respect. In Theban society, a woman who had sex before she got married was seen as damaged goods.

We could have had sex in secret, but nothing remained secret in Thebes for very long, so why take the risk?

I didn't mind, I was happy to wait. I was feeling so comfortable and content with my life that I forgot all about the talking fish.

We picked a date for the wedding and immediately King Creon tried to take control.

He presented us with a ludicrous

guest-list of over two thousand people, most of them foreign VIPs.

He wanted the ceremony to take place in a golden palace that he was having built, and he'd imported hundreds of cockatoos for the occasion (As decoration, not to eat).

Both Megara and I felt that things were getting out of hand. We both wanted as little fuss as possible. But already the market stalls of Thebes were covered in royal wedding merchandise, all of it manufactured and promoted by the enterprising Xylopraxes.

Suddenly, it felt like we were turning into everyone's meal ticket. Megara actually sought out the profiteering Xylopraxes and gave him a piece of her mind. She stormed into his private chambers and gave him a mouthful of profanity that you'd have been proud of.

It got to the stage where, ideally, we'd rather have called off the whole pantomime and just lived together. We really weren't sure we could be bothered to marry. But that would have meant flouting public morals and Megara might have been stoned to death.

Not a risk we had to run, eh, Bessie? The worst we had to endure was disapproving looks from Mrs. McCafferty.

In the end, we told Creon, very firmly, that it was going to be a very small wedding and that *we* would be paying for it.

So the King did not get the spectacular royal wedding that he needed to divert attention away from all the starving citizens and disappearing critics.

Instead, there was a tasteful, understated ceremony on the riverbank – at the same spot where Megara and I had thrown stones and discovered that we didn't hate each other.

The only guests were a few of Megara's friends and her parents.

I invited my parents, but they declined.

I even went to visit them to try to persuade them, though that was a waste of time.

My mother was still too angry with me to countenance coming and Amphitryon, the General, just sat, silent, in his favourite chair, staring into the fire.

It was sad. But there was nothing more I could do.

As well as the contentment of married life, I quickly discovered the satisfaction of having a job.

Creon commissioned me – probably for P.R. purposes – to rebuild the east side of Thebes, which had been burnt down by rioters.

I set about replacing the charred remains of the slums with properly constructed homes at prices that even poor people could afford.

I had everything I could wish for. I had love, a home and a purpose.

Within 3 years, we had 2 children. A boy and a girl. Parus and Lena. In the versions of the legend where their names were recorded, guess what, the legend was wrong!

Both of them were beautiful and both of them were constant laughers. It was lovely. They laughed like a pair of gurgling brooks.

Megara suffered from asthma and both kids had inherited this condition, something that I found hugely reassuring because it meant they ~~also~~ almost certainly weren't demi-gods.

I wouldn't have wanted them to inherit that.

I wanted them to be normal kids. Even if that meant they were fragile.

~~To stand~~ I'm finding this quite ~~diff~~ painful, Bessie.

We employed no help, to begin with, as Megara had hated being raised by servants.

But, when the children hit the ages of four and five, she started to find them exhausting and her health began to suffer.

I tried ~~to~~ take a wee bit more of the load (Yup, you're probably laughing) but Megara got so tired that eventually she could barely string two words together, or two thoughts.

It all came to a head one morning, when she failed to notice that the toy that Paris and Lena were playing with was, in fact, a live scorpion.

Poor Megara was appalled by her negligence. Now, at last, she agreed to taking on some help. We interviewed lots of applicants, but none of them felt quite right.

But then an elderly woman with sad, brown eyes presented herself at the gates of our house. She said her name was Claxa and she'd heard that we were looking for staff.

We asked if she'd had experience of children.

"I had a son," she answered. "And I raised my sister's kids, a boy and a girl."

She was much older than the other applicants, but she had a calm, reassuring presence, so she started work the next day.

Claxa's arrival transformed our lives. The kids adored her and, although Megara still spent a lot of time with them, she now had more time to rest and more room to be herself again.

Everything was peachy, as you would say. Too peachy.

A few months after Claxa joined us, Amphitryon died.

It wasn't a huge shock because, the last time that I'd seen my father, he had the air of someone who'd had enough. So I think he died because he just stopped living.

My mother retreated into hysterics – most of Thebes could hear her – so there was only me to organise the necessary arrangements.

After a little arm-twisting, the King agreed to give Amphitryon a state burial – with full military honours. He could hardly do anything less, given how often my father had saved the city from invasion.

There were a lot of eulogies at the funeral, from former comrades who praised Amphitryon's courage and recalled funny things that he'd said.

I could sense the mourners looking at me and wondering if I was going to speak. But I couldn't think of

anything to say.
So I just listened to the speeches with my head bowed, as Megara squeezed my hand.
The final – and longest – eulogy came from Creon. The King told many stories, most of which were really about himself.
As he rambled through his egocentric bullshit, I found my thoughts drifting back to those very early years.
For some reason, I kept replaying the memory of my favourite cow being slaughtered by the High Priestess, and my father telling me that everything would be alright.
There was nothing else he could say, I suppose. He was probably as frightened as I was.
The funeral felt like a chore. But once it was done, life got back to normal. I thought I was OK, I really did.
By the end, Amphitryon had shrunk to such a small part of my life. And I had a new life now. A great life. I would arrive

home from work in the mid-afternoon and the kids would charge towards me in a little avalanche of affection.

I did everything that a father is supposed to do. And I did it all joyfully.

Much of the time, I was stretched out on the floor. I played incessantly with them, visiting their imaginary worlds.

They saw me as their friend and climbing frame.

I made up stories for them and listened to their stories. When they hurt themselves, I made upbeat noises to convince them they were alright.

I encouraged them, patiently, as they played random tunes on wind instruments.

I told them not to pat strange dogs, until the dog showed that it wanted to be their friend.

I did everything in my power to show them that the world was a good place and that it was theirs to explore.

I was a normal, ordinary Dad. It was liberating. I'd never been ordinary or normal before.

It was also the last time I felt that way. Until here. (Take a bow, Bessie)

I was good with kids back then. But now? Well, I just get nervous around them. You're often remarked on it, telling me that they don't bite.

Though you did once tell me that just before the kid bit you, do you remember? Sorry. But it *was* funny.

So, you're wondering what went wrong? Why didn't my idyllic family life last?

Well, deep down — very deep down — I think part of me questioned whether my happiness was *really* deserved.

Perhaps that's why I started drinking again.

But fear might have played a part as well.

At our first encounter, Zeus had said that I would be punished once I was happy enough. By finding happiness, had I merely set that clock ticking? Was a target on my back?

Or perhaps none of it had anything to do with Zeus, none of the misery.

Perhaps it was just me. All me.

Crazy, isn't it, Bessie? That someone could live so long and understand himself so little.

It started with the occasional night out.

I'd come home a wee bit tipsy and Megara would tease me about how I was a soppy drunk, all sentimental and repetitive.

Gradually, however, the drinking bouts became longer and heavier.

I toured the taverns attracting a new entourage of hangers-on and arse-lickers.

It seemed I'd lost none of my stardom, so every pissed wanker in Thebes wanted to buy me a drink.

To begin with, Megara put up with these all-nighters. I think she felt that, for some reason, I needed to let off steam.

She loved me — so she was prepared to give me the benefit of the doubt.

But her attitude changed once I started coming home so drunk that I became belligerent.

She told me that I could sleep in the spare room until I decided to grow up.

"When you do stumble in", she said "try not to crash about so much. It frightens the kids."

Stupidly, I carried on boozing and then passing out in the spare room. I resented being judged, so I wasn't prepared to back down.

No doubt you'll recognise the stubborn streak — though not the drinking. You've never seen me touch as much as a shandy.

I haven't had a drop for thousands of years. I don't miss it.

One morning, or it might have been the afternoon, I woke up to find that the wall of the spare room had a big hole in it.

The door had been ripped off its hinges and was lying on the floor.

The floor was carpeted with pieces of broken ornaments.

It looked like a tornado had passed through.

I became aware that Claxa was in the far corner of the room, sweeping up fragments of china.

"What happened here?" I mumbled.

She fixed me with a bright, gleaming stare.

"It's impertinent to stare" I told her.

"This was all you" she said. "You were like an animal. You shouldn't drink."

Again, I told her not to stare.

"I didn't frighten the children, did I?"

She shook her head and muttered something that I presumed was criticism.

"I can stop any time I like" I informed her.

"The children are away" she said "With the mistress. Visiting her Aunt in the hills"

"Oh yes, I remember now" I lied.

Claxa chuckled sardonically.

"You remember nothing. The wine has stolen your brain"

I didn't appreciate being criticised by the help so, for a second time, I told her that I was a social drinker and that I could stop whenever I wanted to.

"But you don't want to. You don't

care. About anything. Or anyone. People are just insects to you... ..Sir"

If it had been purely my choice I'd have sacked her on the spot. But Megara relied on her and the children worshipped her.

What did it matter if she didn't approve of me?

I could put up with all the sideways glances and the sharp edge that she could put on the word 'sir'.

She was nothing to me.

That was my reasoning. That's how big a prick I was, Bessie.

Claxa had sounded the same warning about my drinking that I'd heard from my poor, terrified brother.

Pride prevented me from seeing that, I suppose. It leads to so many acts of rank stupidity and self-harm.

Of course, if I'd only harmed myself, then I'd be able to live with it.

But that's not the case.

And now I've arrived at the moment that I have been dreading.

I think my only hope of getting through this is to set down the facts and nothing more.

You may think me to be cold and inhuman, but it's the only way.

As I mentioned earlier, the versions of the myth where I killed my wife are factually wrong. I don't know how that distortion crept in.

In some ways, it might have been better if I had killed her because what I did to Megara was worse than murdering her.

Already, I'm pouring with sweat.

These are the events, as I remember them – in fragments.

Megara and the children returned from their holiday in the hills.

They were in high spirits, though the kids had picked up colds.

My memory is that, for the next few nights I stayed home.

I have a memory of playing hide-and-seek in the garden. It was summer and the evenings were long.

Then I went out on the biggest bender so far.

I started in the early afternoon. I have no memory of anything that happened after the fifth or sixth tavern.

The next morning, I was woken up by nextdoor's cockerel, so it must have been shortly after dawn.

I could hear no movement in the house.

I was on the floor of the spare room. Once again, it was littered with fragments of broken porcelain. A couple of chairs had been broken into bits, but the damage didn't look as bad as in the previous episode.

The silence filled me with an eerie foreboding, so I got to my feet, groggily, and decided to check on the children.

The door to the nursery was wide open.

There were some breakages in

the nursery.

The door to their bedroom was also wide open.

I went in.

I'm not going to describe what I saw.

For your sake and for mine.

All I will say is that there was not a mark on them. They looked as if they were asleep. Two sleeping angels.

There was a pillow on the floor. I have a memory of feeling dizzy. I may have been sick, I'm not sure.

I have a memory of running out of the house.

I have no memory of calling for help or raising the alarm.

I just remember running. I think I ran for the entire day, and for several days after that – until I was the other side of the mountains, at least two hundred miles from Thebes.

I never went back.

It's as impossible for me to describe the emotions I was experiencing as it would be for you to imagine them.

Sometimes words just can't do the job. 'Horror.' 'Despair.' 'Agony'. These are just empty nouns. There is no term for what I was feeling in the decades that followed.

It all seems like a distant nightmare now, but it can still find me.

A few weeks ago, I was sitting in the kitchen doing some work on the laptop.

All of a sudden, I heard laughter and great whoops of excitement. The Andersons were getting a visit from their grandchildren — you've met them, lovely kids, a five-year old boy and a six-year old girl.

After about an hour, their father took them out into the garden, probably so they could let off a bit of steam. They're lively kids, they'd probably been fed a lot of cake by Margaret and were starting to bounce on the furniture.

'Children and furniture are natural enemies.' That's one of your maxims, isn't it.

At first, I quite enjoyed the sound of the kids playing with their father. Screams of ecstatic laughter drifted through the window, along with gurgles of pleasure as they threw themselves at their Dad in a game that seemed to involve a lot of dragons and robots.

It was a pleasant sound – the sound of children having fun with a parent, a sound full of love and joy.

But, gradually, insidiously, it began to fill me with a mixture of self-disgust and wild rage.

What was wrong with me? What sort of animals is driven into a fury by the happiness of others? It was obscene and yet the anger was irressistible; it kept growing and growing until suddenly I was pounding the laptop with my fists, smashing it relentlessly into wee tiny fragments!

It was all over in a few seconds. I sat there, staring at the pulverised corpse of a computer and despising myself even more.

Out of blind panic, I swept up the bits and then told you that it had been stolen. I didn't want to have to explain my rage.

Later, I bagged up the wreckage of the laptop and chucked it in the River Findhorn.

Not very green, I know, but I wasn't thinking straight.

According to the legend, after the killings the goddess Athena took pity on me and restored my sanity.

That would have been nice.

In reality, I just ran.

And that's what I did after I'd dumped my mutilated laptop into the river.

I ran as far as Burghead. I sprinted every mile, flat out, non-stop, like a man trying to outrun himself.

When I fled Thebes, I ran for weeks, ran like a desparate maniac, avoiding human contact.

If I saw people, or heard voices, I either just ran faster or I hid. It was clear to me that I was some kind of abomination against Nature – that's what I had become. So I had to be destroyed; there was no other course of action.

Looking back, I can see that there was comedy in my futile attempts to self-destruct.

I tried everything, every conceivable way, to terminate my existence. I repeatedly threw myself into rivers, opened my mouth and let the water fill my lungs until I blacked out.

But always, somehow, I woke up, wet but undamaged, on the riverbank.

I tried drowning myself in the ocean, but each time the waves chucked my unconscious body on to the shore, as if I was some rejected piece of rubbish.

On the many occasions when I tried to incinerate myself, I discovered that, fundamentally, my body wouldn't burn.

There was some singeing and scorching, but only at a superficial level.

Whenever I threw myself off cliffs, or down ravines, not a bone was broken.

If I slashed an artery, I bled for a few minutes, but then the blood would start to clot and the wound would start to heal.

Poisons had no permanent effect. They simply got flushed out of my body (often, before I could reach a suitable toilet-spot)

Even disembowelling myself – though very painful – proved ineffective. Apparently, there were some organs that a demi-god could manage without. Or I simply grew new ones.

This grim farce lasted for many years. In between the slapstick attempts at suicide, I foraged in the woods for food and, at night, I slept in caves.

Usually, the caves stank of bat-shit. So did I, I expect.

One morning, I was walking through some woods, weeping with quiet frustration, when an extremely large black bear came crashing through the undergrowth, heading straight towards me.

At last, I thought, this creature can despatch me once and for all. Bears eat pretty much everything, so there would be no trace of me left behind to further pollute the world.

I wouldn't defend myself. I just kept my arms by my side and waited for the bear to slam into me.

He was accelerating towards me with a definite sense of purpose, this was *not* a bluff charge, I felt *sure* that he was about to attack *me*.

But, at the last moment, just a few feet away from me, the bear suddenly slid to a halt, reared up on its hind legs so that it towered over me and then giggled!

"When are you going to get the message, Muscles?" said the bear.

Before I could even *think* of a response, the bear dropped back down on to all fours, turned and ran off through the trees, cackling with laughter.

I was too stunned to call after

Him. Besides, what would have been the point?

I had got the message now. Clearly, Zeus was not going to allow me to kill myself. He was not prepared to let me decide my own fate.

Or perhaps he was simply trying to make me understand that it was physically impossible for me to cease existing.

From my point of view, it didn't really matter either way. Whatever the truth, there was obviously no exit that I could engineer. Any release would be at the whim of the laughing bear.

I should have guessed that the bear was Him. It was ludicrously big and glossy.

You and I have never really talked about God, have we Bessie. On reflection, that's probably just as well because I wo

Well, that was annoying.
I was interrupted by the sound of someone with their finger glued to the doorbell.

They kept ringing it non-stop and, at first, I was determined not to respond. But then I panicked. What if it was an emergency? What if there was important news from the hospital? It might not be another journalist.

But it was. This one was a tenacious young woman called Lorraine with a permanent, blindingly white smile and a tendency to over-use the word 'literally'.

She spoke at great speed, like someone who'd taken cocaine (though I suspect she'd have no need of cocaine)

She said that a lot of rumours were circulating about "the giant who is immune to fire," but that her paper would let me tell my own story. For 'big money'.

I told Lorraine that I was about to literally slam the door in her face.

You'd have been proud of me.
I learnt from a master, eh?

Of course she won't give up. Those people never do, I know that from experience.

In the 1930s, by chance, I happened to be in a New York grocery store when the storekeeper got into an argument with a couple of men who worked for Lucky Luciano.

When the men started to beat the tiny storekeeper I intervened and, to cut a long story short, I ended up being strafed by machine-guns.

The fact that I managed to survive all the bullets and hospitalise my assailants, inevitably, made me a very hot news story.

Big money offers came flooding in. There was a very big offer from the New York Times. And an even bigger one from Lucky Luciano.

Lucky took it very personally when I turned down the chance to become his bodyguard. In the end, I grew tired of being pursued by reporters and a psychopathic gangster, so I left the Big Apple.

whenever I've been caught up in confrontations, I've always tried to defend the weak and, if possible, protect lives.

I know that nothing can ever atone for what I did.

I'll never be able to balance that ledger.

But I've done my best to behave like a decent man, albeit one with an obscene past.

For the first few hundred years after my flight from Thebes, I suppose I was in shock – a kind of P.T.S.D.

I continued to shun human contact and live in caves.

In a dream-like state, I drifted across continents, a dishevelled, dazed hermit.

Sometimes, if someone got a glimpse of me, it would trigger wild rumours about some gigantic bear-man.

It's possible, I think, that the Yeti is me. I certainly remember spooking some herdsmen in the Himalayas.

Slowly – very, very slowly, I began to re-enter the world.

I think the turning point was the dog.

It just appeared from nowhere. I was trudging through some scrubland in North Africa, when this scruffy brown mongrel started pestering me for food.

No matter how often I chased that mutt away, it would return to follow me, with its tail wagging and its mouth hanging open in a dopey grin.

In the end, I gave in and let it become my companion. It slept alongside me and became tuned to my every move.

The funny thing is, I never even bothered to give it a name. I don't remember ever having to _call_ it, because it was never more than a few yards away.

The daily routines of life with a dog – the feeding, the stroking, the relaxingly pointless throwing of sticks – all somehow inched me back towards a semblance of dignity.

Actually, I'm not sure that dignity is the right word, but it'll have to do.

Once I'd rejoined civilisation (that's not the right word either) I quickly became aware of how the story of Heracles had got completely out of control.

It had exploded into a nonsensical piece of popular entertainment. Most absurdly of all, the man who had killed his children had been turned into a hero!

How the hell does that work? Their version of Heracles never really seemed to feel anything. He just went around doing stuff. He was barely <u>one</u>-dimensional.

Eventually, I managed to regard <u>that</u> Heracles – the all-action superhero – as something that had nothing to do with me.

That Heracles was a concoction. My real story would remain a secret inside my head.

Until now.

Until now, I never wanted, or needed, to tell that story to anyone else.

I'm hoping you'll believe it. I'm not sure that I would.

Incidentally, maybe now you'll understand why I got so irritable when we were baby-sitting your nieces and they insisted on watching their favourite cartoon.

The Disney version of me is a moron. So that's why I went and sat in the kitchen.

And in case you're worrying about it — because you do get uncharacteristically sentimental about dogs — my little brown mongrel lived to a ripe old age and died, peacefully, in my arms.

The clock's outracing me again. I'm due at the hospital to take over from Ross.

You've got me as company for the night-shift.

According to the last text, the doctors feel that your condition has improved very slightly.

I suppose that's something, though it won't still the swarm of possibilities in my mind.

I can't begin to describe how terrified I am. I can taste the fear, like fine metal on my tongue.

You have to wake up, Bessie.
I'm on my way, please wake up.

1st December

3.30 am.

OK, so, things may turn a bit frantic now, because I'm going to have to greatly increase my writing speed.

I'd hoped to have a day or so to complete this but I'm suddenly on a very tight ~~deadli~~ deadline, thanks to the events of last night which were truly extraordinary by any measure.

I got home from the hospital about an hour ago, but my pulse is still racing at a speed which, for a normal person, would be quite dangerous.

There's no time for me to think and plan, so I'm just going to let this tumble out of me in chronological order.

Apologies if it turns chaotic.

So, I left the house at 8.15

yesterday evening — slightly delayed because Lorraine had blocked our drive with her car.

She said she'd move it, <u>if</u> I agreed to an interview.

But I simply picked it up at the front and rolled it across to the other side of the road.

She went a wee bit pale.

I got to the hospital shortly after 8.30. Your condition was about the same, but your brother was fizzing with anger.

"They've put that little bastard, Ballantyne, in the next room to hers! Can you believe that?"

Everyone in the waiting area was watching him as he paced back and forth like a caged animal.

"He went into that school with a can of petrol, for fuck's sake! They reckon he might have locked the gym doors! I could kill him!"

I expained to him that Billy

had been suffering from hallucinations.
"He may have been hearing voices" I said "He might not be responsible for his actions."

Ross didn't seem convinced. But I could hardly tell him that Billy was the puppet of an immortal narcissist.

"Why did they move him?"

"Oh, I dunno" Ross muttered "He's got complications or something"

"Complications?"

"Yeh, let's hope it's nothing trivial"

I promised Ross that I'd contact him if there was any change to your condition and then I gave him a hug. (Don't worry, I didn't hurt him)

Once he was gone, I settled down in the chair next to your bed and started burbling bits of gossip and god knows what.

It was banal stuff – perhaps you were better off being unconscious – but I had no idea what to talk about. After about half-an-hour, your medical team asked if I'd wait outside for a few moments while they ran some tests.

I drifted up and down the corridor, aimlessly, and then found myself peering through a small window in the door to Billy's room.

There was nobody with him. He looked so frail and lonely. It didn't seem right.

So I went in to sit with him for a few minutes.

He was asleep, probably sedated, but his face looked pinched, as if he was in the middle of a bad dream.

I held his hand. Just so he'd know someone was there.

And I spoke to him, softly. I told him that he was not to blame for anything.

I told him that he was going to be alright (even though I had no real evidence for that)

I said the kind of stuff that you say at a hospital bedside.

It's almost certain that he couldn't hear a word of it. I knew that, but I kept going because it was making *me* feel better.

I was in the process of telling the unconscious Billy that I didn't think the white stag would be bothering him any more, when I was interrupted by a familiar voice.

"What the fuck are you doing in here? You shouldn't be in here, pal"

"I was just keeping your son company" I explained.

"I was out front having a smoke, that's all, I wasn't far"

Mr. Ballantyne hovered in the doorway, leaning precariously on a crutch.

"It's not easy for me. Some bastard broke my leg."

For a moment, I wondered if he was being ironic; but then I realized he was not the kind of person who'd use irony. He just hadn't recognised me as the big bastard in question.

In fact, he looked as if he was having some trouble getting me in focus.

"I was not very far" he said ~~[illegible]~~, as he hobbled to the chair on the far side of Billy's bed.

"I ~~[illegible] not allowed a wee smoke~~

"This is a free country, isn't it? Is a man not allowed to pop out for a wee smoke now?"

He broke off to swear at the chair for being the wrong height.

"Fuck you, chair" he muttered, as he carefully lowered himself into it.

"What are Billy's complications?" I asked.

At first, he didn't answer, but then he murmured "Chest... always had a weak chest.. like his Mum"

For a few moments, he sat staring hard at the floor, as if it had let him down in some way.

To my bewilderment, I realised that I was starting to feel some sympathy towards this apology for a man.

Again, with no evidence to support it, I offered reassurance.

"Don't worry. He'll be OK. He'll pull through."

"If he doesn't I'll be sueing this hospital" came the reply.

As I opened the door to leave, Mr. Ballantyne let out a strangled little sound.

"Sorry", I said "I didn't quite catch that."

"Thanks" he croaked "..thanks for..y'know... carrying my boy out of the fire"

"My pleasure", I replied.

"Those firemen were useless wankers" he said, nodding his head. "I'm sueing *them* for certain. And the school. You should do the same, pal. You and the wee lass in the coma"

I thanked him for his concern and left.

Once I got back to your room, two young doctors gave me an update on your condition. You were stable, they were cautiously optimistic, long way to go, not out of the woods, etcetera.

I asked a few questions, but they said it'd be better if I put them to the Consultant.

After they'd gone, I settled into the chair and took hold of your hand.

For some reason, I started talking about the moment when we met, or rather the moments before we met.

I told you the real reason why I got off that bus in Forres. There's no way of knowing if you could hear the story I told you. So here it is again, in case you couldn't.

I had bought a ticket to Inverness, but at Aberdeen a middle-aged man boarded the bus and sat in the seat next to me.

He was the chatty type and, within about five minutes, I realised that I was trapped with the most boring man I'd ever met – and that's across a couple of millenia.

His name was Nigel Keen ("Keen by name, keen by nature") and, like all true bores, he mistook silence for fascination; because most bores are rampant egoists (as you have often pointed out, when you're briefing me on a meeting of the School Governers)

For the first half-hour, he talked me through the iniquities of the 'broadband ~~postcode~~ postcode lottery'. Then it was BBC bias. Then it was speedbumps, then it was BBC bias again and how the word 'gay' had been hijacked.

Then it was speed limits and all the letters he'd written to the Ministry For So-Called Transport.

The more he spoke, the further away Inverness seemed to get.

It wasn't just the content of what he said that drained you of hope, it was also his voice – a numbing nasal drone which, for some reason, made me picture a wasp trapped in a jamjar.

No other seats became available, so by the time the bus reached Forres I only had two choices – get off, or kill him.

It was, as I remember it, a rather grey afternoon and so I wasn't planning to stop in Forres very long.

But then I caught sight of you, gesticulating fiercely at a man wearing a fluorescent tabard.

I was not planning to get involved, until the man started to get louder and more aggressive. I sensed that his anger was about to turn physical, so I decided to intervene – or, as you put it at the time, 'interfere'.

I remember being struck by the spark in your eyes and impressed by how imaginative your swearing was. (And still is!)

I don't know why I never got round to telling you about Nigel. I think I'd half-forgotten him. The story got forced out by the more colourful episode of our first encounter, with you lambasting me in the middle of the High Street.

That's the anecdote that we always end~~ing~~ up trotting out at dinner-parties, isn't it. That's the crowd-pleaser. How it all began. You and me. But there would have been no you and me without Nigel. Or, I suppose, the chap in the tabard.

Our fates hinge on such tiny events. I wonder, sometimes, if it's at all possible that Zeus could have made that awful man step on to that bus? Does it all join up? Or is it all chaos?

Either way, we owe Nigel a lot.

God, Bessie, I don't know why I'm blethering on about how I blethered to you about Nigel.

It's hardly important. But I've not the time to work out what I should omit, so I'm just going to sling it all down and hope for the best.

For an hour or two — time loses its shape in hospital — I told you all sorts of innermost thoughts and feelings that I suspect you'd have teased me about, had you been conscious.

I thanked you. For many things.

I thanked you for accepting me into your life.

I thanked you for rescueing me from desolation.

I thanked you for being so kind and forgiving when I accidentally trod on your foot and broke all those bones.

I said all these thank-yous in the hope that, deep in that darkness, your brain was hitting 'Record'. Perhaps, as you read this part, it's all sounding strangely familiar.

All the time, I held your hand. I didn't care if you knew it was me, I just wanted you to sense that someone was holding your hand. Just as I'd done with Billy.

Around eleven-ish, I think, a middle-aged man in a pin-stripe suit swept into the room, oozing self-assurance.

"Ah, the heroic Mr Galbraith!" he boomed, in a rich, bassy voice.

The lights started to shimmer and I must have looked concerned because he joked about someone forgetting to pay the electricity bill.

"Don't worry, Mr. Galbraith. The lights do that sometimes. Good old Victorian wiring."

He moved to the sink to wash his hands. I recognised his face from a large staff photo that greets you as you enter the hospital.

"I'm Doctor Cunningham. See?"

He pointed, whimsically, at the

name-badge on his lapel.

I wasn't sure if I liked him. He came across as a bit of a peacock. For some reason, he reminded me of Nigel Farage.

"Action stations" he suddenly barked. "How are we doing, young lady?"

He picked up your medical charts from the foot of the bed.

"Pretty little thing, isn't she. Ve-ry pretty."

I figured that Dr. Cunningham probably appeared before a lot of tribunals.

He studied your notes for a while, humming cheerfully to himself, and then he started to explain that he was a Neurologist and that he had some news that I might find disturbing.

My pulse accelerated.

Why was the room so hot? What was this news? Was it brain damage? Was that what he was about to tell me? Why was he lowering his voice like that? Why was he addressing me in that solemn tone?

"The thing is, Mr. Galbraith," he began "Young Elizabeth here...isn't really in a coma."

I struggled to take in what he'd told me

"Not in a coma! Then...then what is it? Is it shock, or...or some kind of ...fugue-state or...why is she...she's unconscious!"

His voice softened and grew ~~more serious still,~~ even more serious.

"She's not in a coma...in fact, she's not actually unconscious"

"...Not unconscious?"

"No" he said, gravely. "She's just pretending to be."

My head was swirling by now and I felt dizzy.

"Why...why would she...pretend to be unconscious?" I asked.

"So..." he paused to move a little closer "...so that she wouldn't have to talk to you."

Then he started to giggle and his blue-green eyes began to sparkle and I cursed my own stupidity. That was why the room had become so hot and why the electricity was playing up.

"See?" Zeus chuckled. "I don't just do animals. Last month, I spent a couple of days being George Clooney. And I spent a lot of the sixties being Warren Beatty."

I was furious with myself. I should have realised the moment he walked in that Dr. Cunningham was a merely a body being used a costume.

I should have recognised the swagger in the voice.

Instinctively, I stood up and interposed myself between Zeus and your bed, in an attempt to shield you.

"Seriously?" he laughed. "I could snap you like a twig."

He stepped closer and the lights started to shimmer again.

I stood my ground, which just made him laugh even more.

"Quite the hero, aren't we. Yes, I saw you on the news. You're the talk of...oh, what's this country called again? They all blur into one."

I sat back down in the chair – though not of my own free will – Zeus was controlling my limbs as if I was his action figure.

"You just sit there and behave yourself, Muscles"

I tried to speak, but he had control of my throat as well. It was being gripped so tightly that I could barely breathe.

And you were laying there totally defenceless – a few inches away from a capricious psychopath!

"You know why I'm here" he said in a matter-of-fact tone. "I've sent you various signals that you've chosen to ignore. That's a challenge to my authority. That can't be tolerated."

He came closer and stared into my eyes, as if I was a mystery.

"What are you still doing here, boy? You know how this works by now. We've been doing this long enough. When I decide it's time for you to move on, you move on. Explain yourself"

He released my throat and I

gulped down some air as I fought to marshall my thoughts.

We were at his mercy, so the imperative was not to provoke him.

"I've been.. I'm very sorry" I said, slowly and calmly "I should not have defied you. But I fell in love with this woman."

Zeus pulled a teenager's face. "Oh yuk. She's one woman! There's millions of them out there. It's like shooting fish in a barrel.

"This one's special" I informed him. He looked at you for a few seconds.

"Really? How can you possibly be sure of that? You've only known her for the blink of an eye."

"Twenty years"

"Ex-actly!" he cried. "A blink of an eye, no time at all!"

"I can't move on till I know she's getting better. Please"

"She can't get better till you move on" replied Zeus. "Fact."

As I tried not to panic and

carefully considered what I should say next, I became aware that the beeping of your cardiogram had turned more rapid and the rapidity was increasing fast.

"Are you doing that?" I asked.

"I might be" he mused. Then the bleeps got even faster, and louder.

"How strong do you think her heart is?" Zeus shouted over the din of the cardiogram "She looks quite fit."

The beeping quickened yet again. In an instant, the words leapt out of my mouth.

"I'll go!" I shouted "Leave her alone! I'll go! Stop it, please! I'll move on, I promise!"

Almost instantly, your heartbeat returned to a steady tempo.

For a few moments, I was too emotionally shattered to say anything. He had made me imagine that I'd have to watch as you were murdered. I felt broken.

Eventually, ~~anyway~~ once I could speak, I asked him if you were going to recover.

"Maybe yes, maybe no. We doctors don't like to make predictions." Then he dissolved into giggles. "Do you want ~~to~~ me to check your prostate? I've got rubber gloves"

He was having such fun, the ~~narcissistic~~ narcissistic scumbag.

"And what about poor Billy? Will he be OK?"

"Mind your own business" came the reply.

I probably should have let the matter drop, but I felt responsible for Billy's plight. I was the reason he was struggling for oxygen.

"Why did you choose Billy?" I asked.

"Because he's an idiot" said Zeus. "Idiots are easier to work with. If an animal, or a tree, or a rock tells them to do something, they'll do it. They're easily impressed and they don't ask questions. So I always choose idiots, it saves time"

He paused to pick some fluff from the sleeve of his suit (or rather Dr. Cunningham's suit)

"The downside with idiots is, of

course, the stupidity. They have a tendency to fuck up. The white stag told Billy to set a small fire. It was just meant to crank up the pressure, make you shift your arse. But I don't think Billy quite grasped how flammable petrol is."

He gave a philosophical shrug.

"Still, heigh-ho"

"He's troubled" I suggested, a little warily. I didn't want to annoy Zeus and put you in danger again.

"No, no, he's an idiot" came the correction "he's from a long line of idiots".

At that precise moment, almost as if he'd been waiting outside for a cue, Mr. Ballantyne lurched into the room, bashing the door with his crutch.

"These are fucking stupid doors" he slurred, tottering towards me. He didn't seem to have noticed Dr. Cunningham.

"Listen, pal, can you lend me a few bob? Just so I can nip out and get a wee bottle of something"

He sounded like he'd already had a wee bottle of something.

"Only my boy's really struggling and I can't get through this without a drop of – Jesus Christ, it's hot in here!"

I quickly fished a fiver out of my pocket and handed it over. I know you'd call that 'facilitating' but I wanted to get him out of your room as quickly as possible; because Zeus had a strange look on his face, as if he was weighing up whether to destroy the drunken idiot.

Billy's dad was heading for the door, but then he noticed the stranger.

"Alright, pal? I like the suit. Are you up before the judge?"

He was still laughing at his own joke as I propelled him towards the door. Zeus's expression told me that Mr. Ballantyne might be one remark from oblivion.

"Cheers, pal, you're a gent" he told me, before I pushed him out into the corridor.

Once he'd gone, Zeus started to

shake his head.

"I dunno" he sighed, "what do you make of them, eh?"

I was perplexed.

"What do I make of...who?"

"Humans. What d'you make of 'em?...They're weird, aren't they."

His tone had turned really chatty, which I found no less terrifying.

"You've lived among them, my boy, what makes them tick?"

It seemed very strange to hear a god express bewilderment. Was he winding me up?

He was now standing just a few inches away from you, so, again, in the interests of your safety, I opted for flattery.

"Well, you'd understand them better than me. You're the Supreme Being. You created them."

"No, no, no" he snapped "You're not pinning that one on me. I created Life. Not mankind. No, no, I merely lobbed in all the ingredients, millions of teeny, basic organisms, all swirling around in a big, rich, throbbing soup. Next thing I knew, one of the monkeys had made tools and was bossing everyone around."

Zeus shook his head as he remembered.

"Then he taught himself to ~~speak~~ speak and started eating all the - well, everything! They're like brainy locusts"

Again, I couldn't tell if this was a wind-up.

He seemed to be saying that mankind was not a planned species, a mere accident.

That seemed suspiciously convenient. What's more, I *knew* from bitter experience, that he was a compulsive liar.

Still, he'd triggered dozens of questions in my mind, including one of huge importance to me.

But before I could speak, his mood changed again.

"OK, time's up, time for you to go. Kiss whatshername goodbye and shift, come on, chop-chop"

Suddenly, Zeus looked blurred to me, decidedly out of focus, hazy, because my eyes were filmed by tears.

I couldn't let our story end like that, Bessie. I couldn't abandon you with your body still trapped on that bed and your mind still imprisoned. That would be so cruel, obscene.

So I decided to plead. That was all I had.

"Lord Zeus" I stammered "I..can ..can I..please have some more time to sort out my..arrangements?"

"Arrangements?" he said, arching one eyebrow.

"Yes, arrangements..y'know, legal..affairs."

He looked at me quizzically and I felt sure that he knew I was playing for time. You know how bad I am at bluffing. When have I ever won at poker?

The hope was draining out of me as I waited for an answer.

Zeus stared up at the ceiling. The bastard was milking the suspense. Eventually, he looked me in the eye and grinned.

"...You've got till sundown." He clapped his hands with delight.

"I've always wanted to say that."

Sundown. That gave me about sixteen hours. That was better than nothing. It would give me time to finish writing this and perhaps you would wake up in that time. That was all I really wanted, to see you wake from this dark slumber that had been caused by my stupidity and indecisiveness.

So I thanked Zeus for his mercy, even through the words stuck in my throat.

And if you hadn't woken when his deadline ran out? Well, I'd cross that bridge when it came. Maybe I'd be able to negotiate another extension. Who knows? His moods were so unpredictable.

At that juncture, I had presumed that, having made his ruling, Zeus was about to leave and give us some privacy.

But, to my dismay, he plonked himself down in a chair and started to make himself comfortable.

"Well, this is quite nice really" he declared, resting his feet on the side of your bed. "You and me, we've never really had much quality father-son time, have we."

No, because you've been persecuting me for thousands of years, I thought.

Then he began talking and it felt like he'd never stop.

Most of it was whingeing and self-pity. He seemed to feel that, somehow, he was the victim. God got blamed for everything. How was that fair? Or sensible? It was ridiculous that he was supposed to be dictating the destiny of every single human-being.

"There are billions of the little fuckers!" he exclaimed. "And most of them live unbelievably dull and humdrum lives! How would shaping all their destinies be a good use of my time?"

He started to get very agitated about 'inefficient nonsense' that could be found in various holy books.

"I don't decide 'every leaf that

falls', that would be ludicrous micro-management!"

I nodded, tactfully, in agreement and said that I felt I'd taken up too much of his valuable time, but he didn't take the hint.

"I mean, what do those Imams think I am, a fucking gardener? And don't get me started on predetermination. How could I punish anyone if they were simply acting out the script that I'd written in advance? And think how bor-ing that would be for me?"

That's the main headline concerning the nature of God, my love; it's all about Him. You don't hear that on Thought For The Day.

By now, Zeus had become so worked up that I noticed some sparks fizzing out of the wall-plugs.

"Alright, yes, it's true that, on occasions, I sometimes choose to intervene in the lives of mortals.. if the situation merits it."

"If the situation merits it?" I

echoed.

"Yes" he replied, a little defensively. "Or maybe if I'm bored. But the truth is that, most of the time, I'm an alibi. If I control everything, that gets people off the hook."

He stood up and started pacing around as he fulminated. It was all the fault of the priests! He hated priests; they were self-serving scum who just wanted to frighten everyone.

The room was growing extremely hot and, for a moment, I wondered why no staff had been in to check on you. But then I realized that, despite his protestations, Zeus was probably controlling the nurses.

As I've mentioned, Bessie, he's a liar. Worse than Trump.

"The weather!" he suddenly cried "that's supposed to be down to me. Granted, I created the ingredients, the winds, the dynamics, etcetera, but it's a chaotic, random system that just generates outcomes. I don't bother to rig the outcome. I certainly don't sit around deciding whether to rain off Wimbledon"

At this point, Bessie, I felt extremely torn.

A huge part of me desparately wanted for him to just get the hell out of that room — away from you, away from us.

But, in thousands of years, I had never encountered him in a mood like this; a mood where he was prepared to discuss the details of his divinity.

Foolishly, perhaps, I thought I might get an insight into the great mysteries. I thought I might have a chance to somehow make sense of it all.

So, I'm afraid I couldn't stop asking questions.

"You don't control everything?"

"Nope" replied Zeus.

"OK, so, for example, you didn't cause the earthquake that wrecked my stables?"

"Oh, yeh, no that was me" he ~~co~~ corrected. "Shame about those stables. You probably

would have won some awards for those".
"It's not about awards" I told him.
"Oh right, yeh, 'course."
He was taunting me, that's how small-minded he is.
"But most earthquakes are not me" he explained. "Most earthquakes are geological, apart from a few that are...."
"Recreational?" I offered.
"Yeah" he laughed "Good word."
"Alright, so you don't control every single thing that happens on this planet. Does that apply to the Universe? Y'know, meteors, solar storms, black holes, are they you? Some of them, at least"
His eyes darted towards the ground, as if the question made him feel uncomfortable.
Maybe I should have backed off.
But I didn't.
Story of my life.
"The infinite Universe" I pressed. "You created that. You made the

ingredients for that."

Zeus hesitated, puffing his cheeks.

"Well...erm..."

I couldn't believe my ears. Had God just said 'erm'? He didn't know! There was something beyond his knowledge! He wasn't truly and utterly omniscient, he was just another cog in the wheel! He was staff!

For the first time ever, I had the bastard on the run!

This would need very careful handling. It was important that I didn't let my excitement get the better of me.

I tried to make the enquiry sound as casual as possible.

"So... are there other Gods then?"

Zeus's expression darkened.

"'Other' gods?"

Again, I attempted to make the question sound detached, academic.

"Yes, y'know, gods.. or a god.. who... supervise the cosmos?"

I sensed that I'd made a mistake.

"What's the matter, Heracles?"

he asked, in a cold, flat tone. "Am I not God enough for you? Am I not sufficiently big and powerful? Is that the problem?"

"No, no, no, not at all," I stuttered. His eyes were now shining with a malevolent gleam and I cursed my clumsiness.

"No, Lord Zeus, I.. it's really not important, y'know, I.. um.. I just wondered."

"'Just wondered'?"

The strip-lights started blinking.

"And tell me, Heracles, does an ant ever.. 'just wonder'?"

I didn't understand the question.

"When an ant is crushed .. squished .. beneath someone's boot, does the ant 'wonder' if there exists an owner of an even _bigger_ boot? A boot that can crush the owner of the boot that's crushing him?"

Well, it was quite an interesting philosophical question, but I wasn't going to risk enraging him with a response. For both our sakes.

"Sometimes you have to accept

not knowing" he said - his voice a fraction more relaxed, almost as if he were talking about himself.

Then he turned and headed towards the door.

"You know what you have to do, Heracles" he asserted briskly "If you're still around after the sun's gone down, there will be consequences"

As he reached for the door, it swung open and in walked a female doctor, wearing a crisp white coat and with a stethoscope around her neck.

"Oh for fuck's sake, Lorraine!" I cried. "Give me a break! This is a hospital!"

"Listen, Malcolm, hear me out" she began.

"You're bursting in on a seriously ill woman, it's-"

"Don't worry, out of respect, I haven't brought a photographer. All I need is a few-"

She registered that the man in the pin-stripe suit seemed to be standing very close to her.

"...Are you alright?" she asked.

"Oh yes" replied Zeus, with a grin that I knew spelt trouble.

"The name's Cunningham" he said, pointing at his name-badge. "Doctor Cunningham."

He seemed to be modelling his performance on Leslie Phillips.

"This is Lorraine," I explained. "She's not a doctor. She's a journalist."

"Naughty, naughty" Zeus gave her a wink. "You do know it's a serious offence to pass yourself off as a doctor, don't you, young lady?"

Lorraine was still processing the wink.

"However, we'll overlook your little transgression because you are so comely."

"'Comely'?" repeated Lorraine. "What century have you escaped from?"

"All of them" replied Dr. Cunningham who seemed to have grown a few inches taller.

I began to steer Lorraine back towards the door because, though she didn't realize it, she needed to get out of there.

But she was ressisting hard, firing questions at speed. There were rumours I'd been immune to the flames because I'd been wearing some kind of new, fireproof undergarments that had been secretly developed by the Ministry of Defence. Was this true?

I said yes and kept pushing her towards the door. She was halfway through her follow-up question when she was drowned out by Zeus's deepest, manliest bass.

"Lorraine, my dear, you have lovely, alabaster breasts. You remind me of a nymph I once knew."

Lorraine looked at me, and then at him, and then back at me.

"Did he say 'nymph'?"

"He trained back in the 70s" I said. "He's a product of that environment"

I began propelling her towards the door again, but suddenly our path was blocked by Doctor Cunningham.

"Would you like to meet God?" he enquired cheerily.

Lorraine tried to pretend that she wasn't perplexed by the non-sequitur.

"Er...no, because there is no God" she

informed Him. "God's just a construct"

"I like certainty in women" he said "It makes them more alluring."

But Lorraine wasn't listening. "Malcolm, you don't seem to exist in public records at all, can you explain that?"

By now, Zeus was grinning with a wolfish leer that hundreds of unfortunate women had seen through the centuries.

I told Lorraine she should leave immediately, but she was a woman on a mission. She kept repeating that her paper would pay good money.

"You owe it to Bessie" she urged. "It could help with the medical bills"

Well, something snapped inside me. She was using you as leverage. What kind of a jackal sees a human-being in a coma as a commercial opportunity?

She was a scavenger, pure and simple.

"Fine! OK! I'll give you the whole

story!" I yelled.

"Oooh," cooed Dr. Cunningham, "this should be interesting."

"You won't regret this, Malcolm, can we start with the fire and how you survived it?"

"Sure" I said. "The flames didn't harm me because I'm an invulnerable demi-god who's been on this planet for thousands of years"

Lorraine rolled her eyes and let out a weary groan.

"I can vouch for that" said Dr. Cunningham.

"Yeah, yeah, ve-ry funny, fellas. Listen, Malcolm, I'm just trying to do my job here and...and can you tell your friend that he is getting inappropriately close and -Jesus it's boiling in here- and if he doesn't respect my personal space, I'm making an official complaint. Now, either you tell us your story or we'll-"

"Excuse me, Lorraine" interrupted Zeus. "Do you mind if I ask you a question?"

"Oh for.. what now?" she snapped.

"Well, my dear, I was just wondering

...have you ever fantasized about being ravished by a giant swan?"

Lorraine stared at him, her mouth open in astonishment.

"......OK pal, you were warned. That's it. I'm tweeting what you just said"

She quickly got out her phone. "Don't blame me if you get struck off. I signalled that you were being inappropriate"

She was so busy tapping angrily at her phone that she didn't notice that Dr. Cunningham was now floating two feet off the ground.

"Do you like music?" asked Zeus, from nowhere. His tone filled me with foreboding.

"Who's your favourite musician?"

"Elvis fucking Presley" muttered Lorraine, head down, as she continued to tweet.

"A fine choice, my dear. And which song from his extremely impressive repertoire would you say was your personal favourite?"

Lorraine looked up to find that the question about her favourite Elvis Presley song was being put to her by Elvis Presley.

Zeus had transformed himself into the King — the Las Vegas, podgy version, in the rhinestoned white suit with the winged collar.

There was a clatter as Lorraine's phone dropped to the floor.

The poor woman stood rooted to the spot, her jaw hanging slack as she stared at Elvis Presley, who was now hovering several feet above the ground.

I pleaded, politely, with Zeus to stop, but he just kept wiggling his lips and telling Lorraine that she was about to experience his 'hunk-a-hunk of burning love.'

Lorraine was, I think, trying to scream, but no sound was coming from her mouth. And Zeus was gliding through the air towards her. I yelled at him to let her go.

"Can't do that" he replied "Not once the divine loins have started the countdown."

(Those were his *actual* words, I swear, Bessie)

It was a nightmare. Zeus was about to rape someone, right in front of me! And there was nothing I could do!

Suddenly, Lorraine found her voice and began to scream at an ear-piercing pitch as she pointed a trembling finger at Elvis – whose black hair had turned into bright orange flames that were licking up towards the ceiling.

"All part of the show, baby!" roared the King, as he loomed over her.

Within a split-second, there was a loud hiss as the sprinklers came on, followed by the clattering ring of a fire alarm.

The drenched Elvis started hopping around the room in frustration, muttering angrily.

"Shit! I *always* forget about the sprinklers"

We could hear approaching voices and running footsteps, so Elvis instantly became Dr. Cunningham.

The next few moments were complete pandemonium.

Lorraine kept screaming, at full pitch, non-stop, as medical staff burst into the room and dived to switch off the electric sockets.

Nurses deftly unhooked you from the machines and began wheeling your bed out into the dry corridor

"This woman needs sedating!" yelled Dr Cunningham, pushing the screaming Lorraine towards a pair of orderlies.

"Is she staff?" one of them shouted.

"No, no, she's not a doctor. She's a fraud who's defiling the sanctity of that white coat"

The other orderly was looking perplexed.

"I thought you were flying out to Portugal, Dr. Cunningham."

"Patients come first!" proclaimed the good doctor. "That's it, let's get this equipment shifted. Well done everyone! OK team, keep it moving, that's it, splendid!"

With one final hiss, the sprinklers stopped sprinkling. Someone asked what had made them come on.

"He did!" shrieked Lorraine, "Him! He's the Devil!"

But she was pointing into empty space, because Zeus was nowhere to be seen. Dr. Cunningham had disappeared, unnoticed, amid the bedlam.

Several orderlies were now bundling Lorraine out of the room, though she wasn't going quietly. Her arms and legs were flailing jerkily, as if she was being electrocuted.

"It was h-i-i-i-i-m!" she carried on yelling – her voice gradually fading away down the corridor.

And you slept through all of this, my love. Zeus, Lorraine, the sprinklers, the panic; this absurd panto had played out around you and your lovely face had remained completely serene.

Shame really. I think you'd have enjoyed it. It was the kind of black farce that would have got you laughing that wonderful smokey laugh.

I waited in the reception area while the nurses got you settled in a dry bed and a new room.

They offered to get me a change of clothes, but I didn't care about being wet.

Besides, I knew they wouldn't find anything that would fit me.

As I sat waiting, I reflected on the chaotic, sprawling conversation that I'd just had with God.

If the unfortunate Lorraine had not blundered in, I might, possibly, have plucked up the courage to ask Him the question – the terrifying question – that had been burning a hole inside me for so long.

But the chance had gone now.

I became aware that someone was crying.

A very distressed, elderly patient had wandered in. He was shuffling backwards and forwards across the waiting area in a state of manic bewilderment.

There was a dark stain on his pyjamas.

He had wet himself and he was weeping with defeat and humiliation.

Two nurses appeared, all smiles and reassurance.

"There you are, Mr. Thompson, you gave us the slip there."

"I'm sorry" sobbed the old man.

"Oh now, don't you worry. We'll soon have you cleaned up. Anyone can have an accident."

And I watched in admiration as, through their professionalism, composure and kindness, they took a human-being at his lowest ebb and led him back to safety.

With jokes and soothing words and a change of pyjamas, they mended a broken man.

And they do this kind of thing every day, routinely.

That's a lot more heroic than

fighting lions, isn't it.

After about half-an-hour, I was shown into your new room.

It was very like the old one. Same décor, same monitors, same drips, same beeping machines. A doctor assured me that you seemed unaffected by your sudden upheaval.

Up on a high shelf, there was a TV flickering away with the sound off.

It was tuned to some rolling news channel – some kind of political discussion format where everyone was getting angry with each other.

Brexit, almost certainly.

I wanted to turn it off, but I couldn't find the remote and the plug was behind your bank of monitors.

So I left it, shimmering silently in the periphery of my vision.

It didn't matter.

Nothing mattered now, apart from you waking up.

In the stillness, after all

the mayhem, it was a relief to be alone with you again.

I had an overpowering urge to lay down alongside you, but the bed was too narrow.

Also, it looked a wee bit rickety. We don't have a great track record with beds, do we.

Remember the one I broke in Kinlochbervie?

All I did was lie down on it, but it just collapsed beneath me, broken into two halves.

That woman who ran the guest-house looked at us as if we were a pair of sex-fiends.

For an hour or so, I kept talking to you, revisiting shared memories in the hope that something familiar might spark your brain back into normality.

I talked and talked.

You'd have been amazed at how much your Malcolm could find to talk about.

It was a struggle. I tried to keep my voice sounding breezy, but I'm not sure I hid the panic.

I was panicking because I needed to be in two places at the same time – there, in that room with you, and back here at this desk.

I had to complete this account before Zeus's deadline expired. I couldn't abandon you without a full explanation.

Back in Thebes, of course, I deserted Megara instantly, without a word.

A few decades later – while I was working as a labourer in Persia – I met a trader from Thebes. Without revealing my connection to the city, I got him drunk and started asking questions about the Princess.

His grandparents had told him that Megara had always refused to believe that her husband could have killed their children.

They had told him that she'd sat at the same window for many years, waiting for my return.

They had said that my wife was, no doubt, still waiting in the underworld. That's what they'd heard.

Well, I'm not prepared to leave you in the dark, Bessie. (Through you may feel that a letter this long is a wee bit over the top)

From time to time, various medical staff popped their heads around the door. One nurse, rather bizarrely, asked if I'd ordered a pizza delivery.

I don't know when she imagined I would have done that.

And all the while the TV kept flickering away on it's shelf, firing out images of people venting their outrage. Gradually, I found that I was beginning to feel angered by their anger.

What were these red-faced morons so cross about? So some politician had not kept some promise, or the price of something had gone up, or some teachers were teaching some children that their parents' beliefs were stupid. So what? None of this was new.

All their self-righteous fury seemed absurd compared with the rage I was suppressing – my rage at the injustice of your coma – the injustice of our situation.

I know from experience that the way to deal with rage is not to listen to it. But, somehow, all those twisted faces on the TV were making that more difficult.

So I climbed up and pulled the TV off the shelf and wrenched its socket from the wall.

I think that's called a coping mechanism.

Normally, when I find myself in extremely stressful situations I head off to Fortingall and sit staring at that yew tree in the churchyard – possibly the *only* thing that's been living on this planet as long as I have.

You always wondered about my sudden absences, I know, but, often, I'd simply gone to calm myself down by bonding with a tree.

You've often said I'm an 'old hippy'. It turns out I'm a ridicously old hippy.

It's hard to work out exactly how old the tree is because a yew can regenerate itself.

Also, quite a lot of it is missing now, thanks mostly to mankind.

The ancient Celts burnt out its centre as part of their funeral rites. (Or was it the Picts? I lose track of all the tribes)

The Druids hollowed it out to form a processional arch. (I'm fairly sure it was the Druids)

Victorian souvenir-hunters liked to make off with bits of the tree that they would display in their homes.

And, inevitably, because the yew has always been seen as a symbol of longevity and fertility, countless pieces were stolen by morons who wanted to have longer lives and/or longer penises.

Humanity has been whittleing down this tree for centuries. Many tens of centuries.

But it has endured.

It squats, defiantly, in its enclosure, even though it is now just a chaotic tangle of curling, gnarled branches.

I've grown very fond of that tree. Its company, and kinship, has helped me through some tricky moments.

The tree's fame will probably kill it in the end.

Every day, tourists besiege it with their cameras and demean it with their selfies.

I know, Bessie. I'm being snotty. But it's not a place of sanctuary any more.

I'm sorry I never took you to see it. You'd like it. I didn't take you because it was somewhere I went when I didn't trust myself to be around people.

When the next nurse came in to check on you, I told her

that the television's socket had spontaneously ripped itself out of the wall.

My mind was so befuddled that I couldn't come up with anything better. Besides, I didn't really care whether she believed me or not.

My plan was to stay with you until your brother arrived and then I'd dash home to finish writing this. I calculated that I would just manage to beat Zeus's deadline of sundown.

I was trying *not* to think about how on earth I would say goodbye if you were still submerged in a coma.

A sense of exhaustion was slowly creeping through me, a feeling that I've not experienced very often.

To my surprise, I found myself drifting off to sleep for a few moments, before jerking awake.

Various medical staff came and went, all was quiet, until around 2.a.m. I began to fret that the room was getting a wee bit too warm for you.

So I crossed the room to check the controls of the air-conditioning. When I turned around you were standing next to the bed!!!!

And you were smiling at me!! It was the moment I'd been praying for! I felt an electrifying surge of joy course through my body.

You were back! There was that smile! You were out of that bed!

Except that.. you were also still laying in the bed.

There were two of you!
The upright version wagged a finger at me and spoke in the voice of Him.

"What are you still doing here, eh?"

I was too shocked to respond.

"You're supposed to be sorting out those 'arrangements' of yours"

Still, I couldn't respond. The sound of his voice coming out of your mouth felt utterly repellent to me. It was an obscenity.

"Oh come on, stop making that face," he scoffed. "Lighten up! You've got to admit it's pretty impressive, isn't it."

He wiggled your hips at me. "See, sometimes I inhabit a person, sometimes I copy. Though I'm not sure I like having the body of a woman. There's too much going on"

In a moment too quick for my eyes to register, Zeus became the bearded, classical, pain--in-the-arse version.

"That's better" he said. "I don't know how women put up with all that. No wonder they're so moody."

He moved towards me and a wall of heat came with him.

Inside, I was now white-hot with rage. By impersonating you he had found yet another line to cross.

"So, Heracles.." His tone hardened. "Yet more disobedience. I grant you more time specifically to sort out the legal affairs that you seemed so concerned about..."

He shook his head ruefully. "But where do I find you? Exactly where I left you! Still moping over your 'girlfriend' like some lovesick teenager. Pull yourself together! You are the fruit of my loins. Show some fortitude, some dignity! This..wimpish inertia brings you nothing but shame!"

Well, Bessie, there were a lot of things I could have said.

He was lecturing me about shame. He had put both you and Billy into a coma. He had plunged Lorraine into madness. He had ruined my mother's life, and my father's, with a casual rape. He had killed thousands on a whim on many occasions. He had done all of that and yet he had the gall to stand there and tell me that I should be ashamed.

I could have said all that. But I didn't; because at that moment just three words were reverberating through my mind. 'Don't provoke Him.'

Clearly, his mood was extremely dangerous so I promised myself that this time I would not let my emotions get the better of me.

I would ignore his hypocrisies and self-serving inconsistencies and I would remain calm and considered. You needed me to keep a cool head.

So I opted for a strategy of humiliating submission. I apologised, profusely, for having dragged my feet.

I explained that I had hung around a wee bit longer than I'd meant to in order to help get you into this new room. I told him that everything had been something of a shambles because the staff had been at full stretch coping with Lorraine's hysteria.

He frowned, as if I was talking nonsense.

"What?" he snapped.

Very politely, I reminded him about the episode with the flaming Elvis.

"She caused quite a hullabaloo," I said. He continued to frown, so I elaborated. "The, y'know.. the woman who.. you tipped into insanity."

"You'll have to be more specific" he said.

"Lorraine," I prompted. "She.. she.. it doesn't matter"

From his expression, it was clear that once he had sexually assaulted a woman she was old news.

"I'm not interested in your excuses" said Zeus "None of the other demi-gods I've sired give me the problems that you do."

So there were others. I'd always wondered.

"You've been trouble since I

first appeared to you as a magnificent fish. You defied me, insulted me, flouted my authority.. swore at me. It won't do."

He raised his eyebrows quizzically; the suggestion seemed to be that he was waiting for some kind of apology.

"I'm very, very sorry for all my past misdemeanours" I said in as dutiful and filial tone as I could muster.

But this didn't appear to satisfy him.

"It's about respect". His face turned into the face of Marlon Brando. "You don't a-show me no respect" he mumbled. He looked like a perfect facsimile of the Godfather.

Zeus snapped back into his normal shape ('Normal' is not the right word)

"I loved that movie" he chuckled. "I like anything about the Mafia. They're my kind of people. They understand how the world works"

Then his expression suddenly darkened again and he launched into another tirade about my "serial disobedience"

Still, I said nothing. His mood seemed so erratic and volatile and I didn't want to risk a mis-step.

So, even when he started a long, angry list of all the many ways in which I had disappointed him as a son, I just stood there and took it.

You'd have been proud of me, Bessie. He kept ranting at me for about ten minutes, heaping abuse and criticism on me, and yet all the while I exercised self-control and managed to keep my temper.

Until I didn't.

It's funny, the Malcolm that you know would never have snapped. Your Malcolm would have been able to withstand that pressure. He's a man of judgement. He'd have kept his eye on the bigger picture, which was your safety.

But we all present different faces to different people, don't we. With you, I'm Malcolm. But with Him, somehow, I always regress to being Heracles.

And Heracles never knows when to shut up.

I let you down, Bessie. I'm sorry. I let him provoke me to the point where, for a moment, you stopped being my priority and I thought only of myself.

The tipping point came when he branded me an 'embarassment'

"You don't seem to have inherited any of my attributes" he declared. "You don't have any of my charisma. Or style. Or class"

That was it. It was impossible for me to let that one pass.

So I told Zeus that I didn't think rape was very classy. Nor did I think it was particularly classy to sire bastards while pretending to be an Aberdeen Angus.

And it wasn't stylish or classy to have destroyed the sanity of so many women just because he had a hard-on.

Zeus looked genuinely perplexed by the notion that his erection might not be more important than someone else's sanity.

I probably should have left it at that, but my blood was up and I was on a roll.

"You keep banging on about respect, respect is a two-way street" I told him.

He affected a sarcastic, theatrical yawn as I explained that respect had to be earned. A God could not expect to be respected if he did not behave in a moral way.

"Oh here we go" he sighed. "Ok, listen up because I'm not going to repeat this"

He paused for dramatic effect.

".....Humans presume that God

is a good guy because they imagine that the whole of Creation was made specifically for their sole benefit."

I must have looked as if I was struggling to grasp this because he started to talk more slowly.

"Humans..mistake me for a benefactor because I bestowed this world on them as their playground. That's what they think. But it's pure narcissism on their part."

Zeus shook his head in wry amusement.

"This world existed long before they arrived and it will be here long after they're gone... well, unless they blow it up."

I felt a ripple of excitement because I was sure that I'd just spotted a contradiction.

"So...you're saying that.. ..you're not moral?" I confirmed.

"Nope. Never have been. Never will be" he replied, proudly.

"So..if you're not moral....

..why punish? Without a sense of morality..on what basis can you punish?"

Zeus fixed me with a broad relaxed smile.

"I punish you..." he began "to remind you how very small you are. Men have a tendency to forget that. Especially big ones"

He clapped his hands together and motioned me towards the door.

"Alright, that's enough talking. You need to be out of here now, otherwise –"

"And when will all this stop?" I interjected.

"I'm sorry, you've lost me"

"When will it all stop? For me?" This was just one of the many questions that were now swirling around inside my mind.

"Not just the punishment" I went on "I mean, all of it, all of this..this ridiculous..farcical indestructibility..this.."

Zeus threw his arms up in exasperation

"I've never known anyone whinge so much about being immortal."
He looked at me incredulously.
"Are you seriously telling me that you'd rather be dead?"
"Yes.. if it means that the only alternative is living on, eternally, without her"
He peered at you as if you were some kind of specimen.
"You're kidding me, right? You'd rather have a future as worm-food than lose her?"
I nodded, dumbly.
"There's an infinity of women out there."
I didn't respond. Suddenly, I felt extremely tired.
"Why would you want to leave the party? Life is good. It's something to do. Nothingness is so.. samey. I can't believe you want this to stop."
"I've wanted it to stop since the day I left Thebes" I muttered.
He expressed his bewilderment and I felt bewildered by his

bewilderment.

How could He fail to understand what I meant?

Or was he just being deliberately thick?

You shouldn't have to spell things out for a God, should you.

Then it occured to me that he was simply trying to force me to say it — just to increase my pain.

"Because of the children" I stated.

"Oh, them" he said dismissively. "OK, Muscles, we've got sidetracked again, enough chitter-chatter, it's time for you to obey my command and say goodbye to this—"

And then, to his surprise, I interrupted him loud and clear. I interrupted Zeus with the question — the question that haunted me through all of my wanderings — the question that, up until that moment, I had never summoned up the bravery to ask.

But his casual dismissal of the children had ~~emboldened~~ emboldened me. So now I would have an answer; no matter how terrible that answer might be.

"The madness..." I began "..was that..was that..purely..all me? Or..or did..."

Zeus furrowed his eyebrows. "Are you asking me if I made you kill your kids?"

I stared at the floor. I didn't want to risk eye-contact.

It felt like time had stopped. Everything, every aspect of my existence, seemed to have been compressed and crushed into one dark, particular question.

"Well, well, well" he said "this is a very pretty turn of events. At least have the guts to look me in the eye when you ask me this stuff."

I looked him in the eyes; they were blazing with malevolence. "I just..need confirmation" I croaked, shaking with the emotion. "I just need to know... whether that was one of your.. ...interventions.. or whether.. it was entirely me."

Zeus got an attack of the giggles.

"The Greeks blamed your nuttiness on Hera, didn't they.. whoever the fuck she was. But you're wondering if it was me, if I'm guilty of infanticide."

His stare had become more intense, so I looked back down at the floor. My heart was pounding as I waited, fearfully, for an answer.

"Back in a tick" he suddenly chirped. "Don't go anywhere."

When I looked up, he had disappeared, but, in an instant he was back again.

Only this time he was not alone.

Standing a few feet behind him – in the gloomy corner of the room – was a short, frail figure who was wrapped in a dirty, tattered grey cloak that reached down to the floor.

The face was shrouded in a hood and the figure's appearance was sufficiently sinister for me to instinctively step across to shield you, guard you, protect you.

"Your girlfriend's in no danger" said Zeus "This is an old friend of yours."

He reached out and tugged the figure forward. "Ring any bells?"

I told him that the hood was obscuring the face.

"Ye-ah... there isn't really a face.. not as such.. on account of the leprosy"

I stared at him in disbelief. "You brought a leper.. into an Intensive Care Unit?"

"Oh, people are so silly about leprosy. It's not very infectious. And they can't infect anyone when they've been dead this long"

"You brought.. a dead leper.. into an I.C.U?"

"Alright, don't get all Health and Safety." He turned to the cowering figure. "Introduce yourself"

The figure retreated a few inches. Zeus lowered his voice.
"Probably a bit traumatised. Must be quite a shock to be suddenly whisked out of the Land of the Dead."
(So that's that big question answered, eh Bessie?)
Zeus urged the hooded figure to step forward, but still it hesitated.
"She's getting on my nerves now" he muttered.
'She?' For a heart-stopping moment, I thought this might be Megara.
That thought must have been written all over my face because Zeus started laughing.
"Don't be scared, it's not the missus" he said, putting on a cockney accent. "Tell him your name"
Her voice was a tiny, quiet rasp.
"Hespia.. though that's not the name you knew me by"
Her voice wasn't familiar.
"Hespia's got something to tell you, haven't you, Hespia?"

Zeus gave a pretend drum-roll. The bastard was enjoying himself. The hooded woman cleared her throat with a deathly rattle.

Even though you were just inches away from me, Bessie, I have never felt more alone. I was about to hear revelations from beyond the grave and the glint in Zeus's eye told me to fear the worst.

Slowly, the woman pointed a skeletal finger towards Him.

"Mighty Zeus...did not kill your children" she muttered.

Now the finger was pointing straight at me.

"You..Heracles...did not kill them"

I felt dizzy and gripped the metal frame of your bed.

"I killed them" she said.

I should have felt shocked, but I felt nothing because I couldn't take it in.

"Tell the man why you killed his kiddywinks" breezed Zeus.

She pointed at me again.

"For my son, Delerion. You didn't know

his name, of course. Why would you? He was nothing to you."

"So, there's your first clue, Heracles. De-ler-ion"

For some reason, Zeus was now speaking in the voice of Chris Tarrant.

"Would you like to phone a friend?"

The shrouded woman had begun to shake.

"He was my only child. He was fourteen when he... he had no life... he was lovely... he..."

In as respectful tone as possible, I told her that I was sorry for her loss, but I didn't know who her Delerion was.

"They conscripted him" she said "He didn't want to join the army"

"Whose army?" I asked.

"The Minyan army"

"Did he die at the Battle of the Crone's Teeth?"

"No. Before then. Though I heard that wasn't a battle"

"No it was more of a massacre, wasn't it, Heracles" added Zeus with a grin.

She ignored Him. I was her sole focus. "He got hurt in an avalanche. He surrendered himself to you"

The broken-shouldered boy! My god, was this all about that poor, doomed boy!

His mother's voice grew firmer. "He was your prisoner, your responsibility. By all the rules of honour, you should have seen that no harm came to him. But you let them slaughter him like an animal. In front of cheering crowds."

I wanted to protest that I'd not been there when her son was sacrificed, but I suppose that was the point she was making.

"You didn't give him a second's thought" she hissed. "He was a nobody, a nothing.. you didn't care."

Her voice dropped back down to a hoarse, hypnotising whisper.

"It took me a year to get to Thebes. Changed my name, so no-one would guess I was Minyan. Then I started asking around. To find the truth. About what happened to my boy"

She shuffled a few painful steps towards me.

"Whoa, not so fast, girl!" mocked Zeus, still lapping up all the entertainment.

The woman let out a thin, wheezing sound which it took a few moments for me to realize was laughter – bitter, sardonic laughter.

"I spent days watching your house. Morning and night. Just waiting for my chance. I knew an opportunity would present itself if I was patient. But love is patient. Love waits."

Although it was so feeble and hoarse, I was starting to detect a tone in her voice that seemed vaguely familiar.

"Once I was inside it was so easy. I could have done it at any time. You were so drunk, so often"

Yes, now the voice was definitely familiar.

"All I had to do was pick the moment...sir"

The way she curdled the word 'sir' was unmistakeable.

I stepped forward and slid back the hood.

The leprosy had stolen much of her face, but the face that was left was still Claxa.

Her one remaining eye stared at me with blazing defiance.

"She's no oil painting, is she" said Zeus, sounding a wee bit bored.

I thought I was going to faint — an experience that I couldn't remember having had before.

My head felt strangely light, so did my stomach. It seemed to me that I was watching the world through some kind of gauze.

My mind couldn't take in the reality of Claxa being a murderer. It made no sense. She had always been so very affectionate with the children.

"They didn't suffer" she whispered. "I drugged them both first." She was struggling to catch her breath.

"I...I used a pillow. That was my weapon"

Every word seemed to be causing her physical pain and part of me would have liked to her to stop. But part of me was transfixed; hypnotised by the horror.

"Killing them wasn't enough to avenge my boy" she continued. "That wouldn't be sufficient torment for you. So I made you believe you'd killed them. All I had to do was smash up a few chairs and vases"

She stared hard at the floor, as if she was replaying the pictures to herself.

"You slept through the whole thing. You came home drunk. I only had to drug the wine that I knew would be your bedtime tipple. You downed gallons"

I opened my mouth to speak

but she already knew the question.
"Why didn't I just cut your throat and spare the children?"
Yes, that would have been a better outcome – for everyone.
But Claxa was nodding slowly because she knew the loophole.
"Well... sir, your throat would probably have healed right up, wouldn't it."
Zeus laughed. "Bright girl, eh? She's not just a pretty face"
He giggled at his own joke.
"Oh come on, big boy, no need to lose your sense of humour."
Claxa shuffled closer until her ravaged face was a few inches from mine. Her voice dropped to a *tiny*, barely audible whisper.
"If I'd killed you, even if I *could* have killed you, I wouldn't have secured justice. Because you'd have been freed from pain."
She muttered the word 'justice' quietly to herself, several times, as she inched even closer. Her

poor face was little more than a skull.

"I needed you to suffer. I thought that knowing I'd caused you intolerable, endless suffering ...would diminish mine."

She lowered her head.

"I was wrong"

At that moment, I suppose, now that I knew the truth, I should have been engulfed by fury.

The murderer of my children was standing before me.

Just a few inches away.

She had framed me and sentenced me to thousands of years of mental torture.

The woman was some kind of monster – an evil witch.

But the fury never arrived. All that I could see was the wreck of a human-being, who had been hollowed out by unendurable pain.

And, like me, she'd had no choice but to endure it.

I understood that.

So I felt no rage.

"The King ordered for your son to be killed" I said, softly. "He was the one who murdered him."

She nodded to herself for a few moments.

"I would have killed him if I could have. But I could never get close enough. As thew years passed he got more and more bodyguards"

"I quite liked Creon" Zeus chipped in. "I liked his attitude"

"Besides.." Claxa paused to catch her breath "..the King only did what Kings do. He had no decency in him."

She slowly pointed a boney finger at me again.

"But *you*.. you should not have been so casual and so cruel. My boy would have expected you to protect him"

She was right, of course. I had made a promise to her son. But the adulation of the crowd had made me forget him.

How stupid I was then.

Hesitantly, I stepped forward and embraced her.

I held her very gently because there was hardly anything of her. She felt like she might break into powder in my arms.

She didn't recoil, in fact, she didn't react at all.

But Zeus was appalled.

"Eurgh, yuk! You're cuddling a leper!"

I ignored him and told Claxa that I was sorry and ashamed that I had let her son die. I told her how uncomplaining and brave he'd been about his broken shoulder.

Zeus was hissing with frustrated puzzlement.

"I didn't bring her here for therapy! This old hag killed your kids! What is *wrong* with you?"

Well, how could he understand, eh Bessie?

What would a God know about grief?

To experience it, a God would

have to make himself powerless – at which point, he'd stop being a God.

I know that the Reverend McCabe would tell me that his God experienced the same grief as humans when he watched Jesus die on the cross.

But Jehovah knows that his son is going to be fit and well again in three days time, so I hardly think that counts.

In that story, God is basically an emotional tourist.

(Perhaps you could make that point next time you bump into the Vicar)

No, a God can't understand loss. Nor the aching, permanent absence that underscores grief.

Even the word 'grief' doesn't really capture an emotion that is incomprehensible and ambiguous and which every individual experiences in a different way; just as the word 'blue' tries to describe a colour that every brain sees in a different shade.

Anyway, the relevance of all this is that the feelings that Claxa and I were sharing as we embraced were making Zeus feel out of his depth.

He felt uncomfortable, possibly even excluded. This was not about Him. So it had to stop.

He clapped his hands together. "Okay, that's it. Hug-A-Leper week is over"

And, in a micro-second, I was embracing the air.

Claxa had vanished.

He'd despatched her back to the Land of the Dead.

"You are such a weirdo" said Zeus.

His discomfort told me that things had not turned out quite the way that he'd expected.

Clearly, he had assumed — or hoped — that I would go to pieces.

He had imagined that I would humiliate myself; that I'd be consumed by lunatic rage once I heard Claxa's revelations.

But, in reality, her words had freed me from the heaviest of my shackles.

So I told him that.

"I'm no longer the man who killed his children" I said.

"We-ll.. you sort of are" he quibbled. "Indirectly, your action ..or inaction, eventually caused their deaths, so... y'know, don't meant to be picky, but them's the facts"

He started chuckling to himself.

"It's hilarious, really. All those thousands of years when you had the wrong end of the stick. In fact, when have you _ever_ had the right end of the stick?"

"You could have told me" I said "Why didn't you put me straight?

"You never asked" he shrugged. "If you'd asked 'Did I _actually_ kill my children?' then.."

I snorted with contempt.

"Besides" he went on "you were

having too good a time being all tragic and self-dramatising"

With a weary sigh, he added "You get that from your mother".

Then, to my extreme consternation, he leant over you once again and studied your face.

What was going through that diseased mind?

You were comatose. Surely even He would draw the line there?

"Is the sex especially good? Is that it?"

I suppressed a strong urge to punch God in the face.

"Because I can't see anything special about her. Look, her nose is wonky"

So I told him that I loved the nose you broke playing hockey, that I loved the totality of you and that you were my best friend.

"You're a cretin" he replied. "You get that from your mother as well"

He pointed disdainfully at you.

"There are millions of these out there"

"No," I informed him "there's only one"
"Whatever."
He stepped away from your bed and then suddenly declared "Alright, that's enough yakkity-yak, I allowed myself to get distracted. I came here to tell you to shift your arse, so shift it."
I reminded him, politely, that he'd promised me that extension – till sundown.
"OK, Mister" he said, in the voice, the exact voice, of John Wayne. "I'm a man of my word. You've got till then to get out this territory. But if I catch you around here after nightfall – or around her – there'll be hell to pay, you got that?"
He stopped mimicking the Duke and glided towards me.
"I mean it. It'll make what's happened so far look like a Quaker's picnic. That'd give you

something new to feel guilty about, if I destroyed whole swathes of... what's this bit called again?"

"Scotland"

"Yeh, Scotland."

I assured him that there'd be no need to destroy an entire country. Come sunset, I would be gone.

"You'd better be" he declared.

He, finally, seemed to be about to leave and I began to feel relieved that you and I would be alone again.

But then he paused by the door and pointed that finger again.

I felt a small jolt of electricity.

"You will be on a different continent by the end of the week. At least.. five thousand miles from here. Do I make myself clear?"

"A different continent" I stammered "Absolutely."

"Don't make me destroy Scotland"

"I won't"

"And you will have no future

contact with Ol' Broken-Nose here. No contact of any kind"

"Understood"

"Don't worry, you can have some private time to say goodbye. I don't want to listen to any drivel"

Though it stuck in my craw, I thanked him.

"You've got five minutes" he said.

"Five minutes?!!!"

"Yep, if you're not out of this hospital by then, I'll flatten everything with a tidal wave or an earthquake or something. Or maybe a firestorm. Yeh, I haven't done one of those for a while"

I fell to my knees — yes, I actually got down on my knees to the scumbag — and I begged and implored him for more time. Just an hour or two, I pleaded. At least till your brother arrived to sit with you.

"Once he's here - and she's not alone - I'll leave for ever" I promised. "I'll go back to the house, sort out my arrangements and, by sunset, I'll be gone, I swear!"

Zeus broke into a wistful smile. "I don't know why I'm so soft on you."

Seriously? Was he taking the piss?

"Normally, I never negotiate. Maybe it's because you're family. I come over all sentimental."

I couldn't detect any irony in his voice, but he's such a compulsive trickster — and his voice is constantly changing — so you can't take anything he says at face value.

Suddenly, he furrowed his eyebrows as if a new thought had occurred.

"These.. 'arrangements' you keep wittering on about.. they're not that stupid letter you've been writing, are they?"

Holy fuck, I thought. What do I say?

It seemed futile to try and lie, but what if he got angry and destroyed my work?

Then you'd be left, abandoned,

with not a word of explanation from me. You would hate Malcolm for what he'd done.

The thought was unbearable.

"There's.. not much about you" I said.

"That's disappointing" he frowned "And a little offensive"

Again, I couldn't tell if he was being serious, so I opted for silence.

"My dear, idiotic Heracles, your tome is full of delusional self-pity and grotesque innacuracy"

"...So you've read it?"

"I don't need to read it." His eyes were twinkling now, as he relished the moment.

"You've never understood how little you understand."

Well, Bessie, he may be right there.

His mood changed yet again; this time to cheerful.

"You write whatever you like" he breezed. "I really don't give a hoot. Let's face it, no-one's going to believe any of it"

"I only need her to believe it" I said softly.

"Hm...she *might* believe it." he mused "She doesn't look very bright"

I know, Bessie, you're right, that's 'fucking rude', but this was not the moment to pick him up on it.

Zeus reached for the handle of the door once more.

"Okay, I'm out of here. There's a nurse in Pediatrics that my loins have taken a bit of a fancy to"

He still hadn't said whether I could sit with you for longer than five minutes, so I pressed him, but with a lot of 'pleases' and quite a bit of grovelling and arse-licking.

It made me feel dirty, but I didn't care. The ends justified the means.

Dignity was a luxury that I could no longer afford.

"*Surely* you can say whatever

needs to be said in five minutes? She won't hear a word of it in any case. You're basically talking to a cabbage"

Again, rude, but not the right time.

I explained that the doctors felt that maybe you could hear and it was important to me that you shouldn't sense you were alone.

"I can ring her brother, but he can't possibly get here in five minutes so–"

"Alright, alright" Zeus interrupted "cut the cackle. You can have a bit more time"

I thanked him profusely.

"You've got ten minutes."

He'd done it me again! Ten!? Ten minutes? I started to protest.

"But, my lord, her brother will–"

"–have to get his skates on. Ten is my final offer. Be out in ten, or Scotland becomes Notland."

He laughed at his own stupid joke as I battled to marshall

my thoughts.

But, before I could open my mouth to protest any more, God winked at me and boomed "Nursey, here I come!"

And then he was gone.

Ten minutes.

Ten minutes to distill twenty years.

This was one more act of cruelty from him. He knew what he was doing. He had saved the worst till last.

What an utter cunt. I know you don't like that word, Bessie, but I can think of no better noun in the circumstances.

In the silence, the bleeping of your machines seemed to be getting louder as I struggled to clear my head.

There was no point getting angry. There was no use in losing time by raging against how little time there was.

This wasn't about me. The Divine Ratbag had won as he always did. Well, I simply had to blot him from my thoughts, you were all that mattered.

I quickly phoned Ross and told him that I had to leave earlier than I'd planned so he'd best set off for the hospital.

Understandably, he began to ask questions and I was a wee bit short with him so can you please apologise to him for that too?

Then I held your hand and desparately, frantically, tried to work out what I needed to say and how I should begin to say it and, as the minutes whooshed past, (at least that's how it felt) the panic swelled and rose inside me and I felt helpless and weak and then something happened that I'd not experienced for a very, very long time.

I started to cry.

I tried to hold it back, but a dam had broken inside me.

Within seconds, I was in floods of tears. They were pouring out of me; tears of grief and fear and release and countless emotions, all blurring into each other.

This was pathetic! I couldn't just blub through our last moments together like some baby!

I tried to speak but all that came out was abysmal sobs and gulps that made it difficult for me to snatch a breath.

Maybe Zeus was right. You were unconscious. What did it matter if I told you things that you probably couldn't hear?

But I still needed to say them. I tried to say the words 'thank you' but I couldn't manage one syllable because my whole body was convulsed with the sobbing and gulping and now I felt like a drowning man, with lungs about to burst, fighting, praying for a chance to grab a precious piece of air.

And just at the point where I began to think that perhaps I <u>wasn't</u> immortal after all, perhaps the overwhelming intensity of this despair could actually kill me, just as I teetered on the edge of that possibility, you gently squeezed my hand, opened your eyes and whispered "Hey Mate."

And then I saw that smile.

For a terrifying moment, I thought that I'd run out of paper!

That would have been too appalling to contemplate.

My train departs in just over an hour and the prospect of having to leave this in an uncompleted version threw me into a total panic!

You'd have laughed, Bessie. I blundered around the house like a mad bull in a china shop and I was just starting to resign myself to writing the last few pages on the back of electricity bills e.t.c when, luckily, I found this stuff underneath a pile of exam papers.

I'm not at my best, I'm afraid.

You may find that this turns <u>even</u> <u>more</u> erratic. I'm having a few problems ~~in the~~ in the clear-thinking department. Sorry.

I'm not even clear in my

own mind what the hell there is to say beyond this single wonderful fact.

You woke up!

For me, that was the only ending that this story needed.

And even though the doctors had predicted it, somehow it felt like a miracle.

That wee hospital room had become a Hell; it had nearly leeched all the hope out of me.

You were only ~~awa~~ awake for a few minutes.

You kept gently squeezing my hand and asking why I was crying. I told you they were tears of joy – which is what they had become.

Then you asked who had dropped a fucking piano on your head.

And I dissolved into even more tears!

I didn't want your last image of me to be a blubbering mess, Bessie, but hearing you swear again was the most beautiful sound imaginable.

It was like listening to a skylark.

Soon, you closed your eyes and drifted away, but this time I knew you were asleep, not comatose.

The snoring was almost as beautiful as the swearing.

As soon as you'd come round I had rung the bell for assistance and, as the minutes ticked past, the room gradually filled with medical staff who started carrying out ~~medical~~ various checks.

It became very crowded. I was much too big for that space, although they kept reassuring me that I wasn't in the way.

They were so quiet and calm. Impressively professional. And as they clustered around your bed, moving with gentle purpose and certainty, I suddenly became aware that I was no longer any use to you.

So I got up and left.

By my reckoning, I was one minute inside Zeus's ten minute limit as I stepped out of the hospital building.

Ideally, I'd have stopped to thank the staff for their work and their kindness, but I couldn't risk Scotland getting annilated just because I had wanted to be polite.

Perhaps you could send them some chocolates or something on my behalf. I'd like them to know how grateful I am.

Writing this is hard enough, but Ralph McGrew's car alarm has started doing that thing again. Stop-start, stop-start. It's like some kind of torture. He keeps saying he'll get it fixed, but he never does.

I will simply have to shut the noise out. I can do that.

Walking out of your room – out of your life – should have felt like a huge dramatic moment, but instead it felt strangely flat.

Weird, isn't it, how often the climaxes end up feeling anti-climactic. The big scenes never quite feel real. Perhaps it's because we've already over--rehearsed them in our minds. Who knows?

In most instances, when you say goodbye to someone for the last time it is very hard to be absolutely, one hundred per-cent certain that you'll *never* see them again.

You may have an instinct, or it may be an extremely high probability, but it is *rarely* a *total* certainty.

Very often in life, you have your final moments together without ever realising it. Until the phone call.

But I knew.

With every step along that hospital corridor, I knew that, in effect, I'd had a bereavment. We were in different worlds now.

There was always going to be a parting of the ways, Bessie.

You'd have grown older while I remained the same age. (Think how maddening that would have become!). In the end, we'd have simply faded from each other's view.

Maybe this is better.

Our farewell was your return from your underworld – a moment of release and elation – so we went out on a high, didn't we. The show had a big finish.

An hour ago, I honestly thought I wouldn't be able to write any more; it felt as if a giant fist had smashed me into a million pieces.

Yet now, an eerie calm has descended on me. I know that there's nothing I can fight against any more.

I suppose this is what they call 'acceptance'.

I can't decide if I like it.

Ross has just texted me.
The doctors are saying they expect you to make a full recovery.
So that is what I shall choose to assume has happened.
As you sit reading this, you are on the mend and you're going to be OK and my selfish hesitations have not left you damaged – at least, not physically.
My great terror is that you stopped reading this many pages ago.
Perhaps you stopped in those first few pages, when you realised how much I'd lied to you over the years.
Or maybe you stopped when I killed Linus, or all those poor Minyan soldiers. Or maybe you simply could not bear to read on once you reached my confession that I'd killed my children.
And who could blame you? But if you did stop, then you won't have discovered that I'm innocent of that crime. All these words might be sitting, unread, unspoken.

That prospect fills me with more dread than any threat that Zeus can conjure up.

Still, I can't control how you will react. In fact, there's nothing I can control so I'd best 'Man up, Wussy' – as it says on your favourite mug.

I just nipped out and dealt with the problem of Ralph McGrew's car alarm. Permanently. I'm afraid my sense of eerie calm didn't extend quite that far.

Don't let McGrew try and pressure you into paying for the damage. He ignored everyone's complaints, so he brought it on himself.

As I left the hospital, I could hear the distant yells of a woman who, as far as I could make out, had just been propositioned by a stag.

In the car park, I was accosted by a ratarsed Mr. Ballantyne who had dumped his crutch and was swaying to music only he could hear.

"Hey! Big Man!" he shouted, from about six inches away, "Come and have a drink wi' me!"

He staggered forwards and put an arm around my shoulder, after several attempts.

"C'mon Big.. Big Man! You're.. you're so big. You're.. you're the size of Wales!"

He dissolved into high-pitched giggles.

"I hate the fucking Welsh", he slurred "Do you hate the Welsh? Of course you do. C'mon, come and have a drink wi' me ... my treat.. though you might have to lend me a wee shilling...c'mon! I'm celebrating!"

I thought about prising his arm from my shoulder, but all his weight was on me and I didn't want him to fall.

"Why have you thrown your crutch on the floor?" I said.

"Because it was fucking asking for it!" came the reply.

I considered walking away

and just letting him crash to the floor. But then I figured that Billy had enough problems without his father sustaining yet more fractures.

"My boy's improving!" he shouted "No thanks to those bastard doctors. Those white coats look stupid, don't they, eh? Eh?"

Firmly, and carefully, I propped him up against a wall. His eyes glazed as he looked into the distance, as if he could see his life receeding from him.

"I wasn't always like this" he mumbled "I used to be... a person."

For a moment, I felt a wee bit sorry for him. Until I remembered that, whatever blows life had dealt him, he had still chosen to be a dickhead.

"Why are you looking so glum?" he slurred.

I have no idea why I told him. Perhap it was because I knew that he wouldn't remember it. or perhaps I just needed to say the words out loud.

So, in a measured tone, I told him that I was looking glum because I was being forced to abandon the woman I love by an infantile and spiteful god and that I was doomed to wander this earth in an unending limbo of loneliness and despair.

"Aye" he said "Tell me about it"

By the time he'd started to list *his* problems, I was already getting into my car.

When I got home, I packed a small suitcase – just a few essentials – and then sat down to write these last few pages.

I'll be taking a train south, to a port. I can't tell you which one, it's better that you don't know.

I've opted not to fly because airport security staff examine your passport a lot more closely.

Also, for a man of my size, airplane seats are torture. I'll head for somewhere distant.

A rainforest, perhaps. Or the centre of a desert. Or the heart of a swarming city.

The sun has just come out and the Firth has turned the most glorious, brilliant blue – which is making this all the more painful.

I am so very tempted to simply stay here with you.

Though, of course, if I did, there would be no here and no you.

Though there is much about Zeus that is ridiculous, his ultimatums have to be taken seriously. Even if he does sound so casual when threatening genocide.

Wherever I head for, Bessie, it's supremely important that you don't try to trace or follow me.

That would be a tragic waste of your time and potential happiness. (And money)

You're a very determined, bright

and resourceful person, but you won't find me.

It's true that it's harder for someone to disappear these days, however I do have thousands of years of experience.

No matter how small the world may have become, there are still caves – both real and figurative.

The time is racing away from and I'm desparately racking my brains for some pithy insights that I could bequeath you. Some pearls of wisdom that might help you make sense of this world's rampant absurdities.

You'd think I'd be able to come up with something, wouldn't you.

After all, I've enjoyed a unique perspective; I've seen empires wax and wane, jungles appear and disappear. I've seen coastlines dance back and forth.

And, in theory, old age brings

wisdom but, in reality, it merely increases the bewilderment.

Of course, I've not experienced 'old age'; I've just lived a long time.

Still, for what it's worth, I'm prepared to take a shot at a few observations.

Obviously, the one thing that I can say for certain is that there is a God. I know because I've met him. So have you, after a fashion.

I'd love to be a fly on the wall when you explain to the good Reverend that yes, there is one god but that he is pagan and a psychopathic wanker who took the piss out of your nose.

The other certainty is that, clearly, there is some form of afterlife. Although Claxa was not a great advertisement for it.

Aside from those two revelations, all I have is opinions. I'm only sad that we won't be able to argue about them over breakfast. Opinion number one: Love does *not* conquer all. Sometimes it can be overpowered by the might of circumstances.

Opinion number two: mankind is always divided into the same consistent percentages.

That is to say that roughly 60 percent are kind, positive, outward-looking people and the other 40 percent are drab, miserable individuals who will *always* feel that they're being betrayed.

In fact, deep down they *want* to be betrayed.

(I know this sounds élitist, Bessie, but, there again, I am a demi-god and Theban aristocrat)

Opinion number three (far from original): Human history sometimes takes a step backwards.

I've seen it so many times now. For centuries, civilisations muddle along making steady advances until, for some weird, unfathomable reason, they forget how to think.

They suddenly decide that a rational mind is a decadence, or a deformity, and surrender entirely to the thrill of their emotions.

Take the Germans, purely as an example. A nation of culture and intellect that had given the world countless scientists, artists and philosophers.

And yet they ended up following a hopeless inadequate who was good at shouting.

But they're just one example, it's a recurring aberration and I can't explain why whole societies collapse into these hysterical episodes.

And, yes, it does look like another one has begun.

Sorry, Bessie, but I suspect you'll be spending many more years shouting at the TV.

My final observation is that – despite what I've just said – if you look at the long arc of history, the wider picture, then daily life has definitely improved for ordinary people.

The ancient world was much more routinely violent, trust me.

You have police forces and public health now and old women no longer get burnt or hanged because they live alone and have a cat.

Similarly, in most countries now, babies don't get killed because they happen to be girls and doctors no longer attempt to cure patients by emptying their bodies of blood.

It would be unthinkable now for people to pay good money to sit in stadiums and watch men stab each other. But that used to be considered as a nice day out.

I'm aware that I'm setting the bar quite low here, Bessie, but I'm just trying to convey the bigger picture.

Despite many disasters along the way, in the round, across the centuries, rationality has won.

So don't lose heart, Bessie. In the end, it's the people like you who prevail.

As for the great mystery of existence, well the nearest I can get to answering *that* is to say life has no meaning any more than a river can be said to have a meaning.

It just flows, that's my take. It has no purpose. It's shaped and re-shaped, moment by moment, by external forces and all it can do is continue to move forward. Until it doesn't.

That's all I've got, I'm afraid. Life is like a river. Abysmal, isn't it?

It reads like something that belongs on a T-shirt.

That's an embarassingly trite effort for someone who has actually had several long chats with God.

Though, to be honest, they provided heat but not much light. Clearly, even our Creator is not in possesion of <u>all</u> the facts.

He knows what He knows and no more — just like the rest of us.

OK, I'm on to my last pen now. I've got through about a dozen. It was never my intention to write this many pages.

At the outset, my plan was to simply tell you the story of who I really was and why I'd had to leave.

But then Zeus told Billy to set fire to the school and you were put into that awful, uncertain darkness and suddenly there was a lot more story that I needed to place on the record.

For a huge amount of it, my love, you were <u>there</u>, like Sleeping Beauty, as the drama played out around you with all its ridiculous sorcery. It's been a busy couple of days.

my train leaves in 28 minutes, but there's no traffic so I can cut it quite fine.

Having to say goodbye like this is bringing home to me that I'm not *so* different from the rest of you. Because this moment is a *normal*, very human one; in the sense that *everyone's* life is a succession of goodbyes.

And everyone's life is composed of many different lives. Heracles and Malcolm are so different in how they view the world that they feel like two entirely separate individuals.

They're not, of course, I know that. It's just how it feels. At least, that's how it felt whenever I was with you.

I imagine that whenever you look back you probably feel similarly disconnected from the wild young Bessie who biked across Europe and once experimented with drugs that are used to tranquilise horses (though I'm presuming that she won't have commited any war crimes)

We all live through so many chapters, perhaps the number is not that important. Perhaps I'm less of a freak than I imagine. Perhaps the only thing that sets me apart is scale.

That and the not dying. But even in that regard, I may soon be less special. A few days ago, I read a piece in the paper by a gerontologist who was arguing that, soon, medical science will be able to defeat all the causes of death.

He seemed confident that, in the forseeable future, human-beings will be able to live for thousands of years.

Well, that will be interesting. It will throw up huge social problems, but I think the greatest challenge for mankind will be psychological.

When your life stretches ahead of you indefinitely, it becomes that much harder to answer the question "What is the point of me?"

Also, think of the crowds. The queues will be terrible.

Christ, I've got 20 minutes!

This is hard, Bessie.

Where do I find the right words?

Endings never seem to satisfy, do they. Perhaps they don't really matter either.

I wish that I had some poetry in me.

As an adolescent, I fancied myself as a wee bit of a poet. I used to write long, turgid, wounded epics and hide them away in my bedroom.

At the Academy in Thebes, Linus repeatedly told me that I had 'the soul of a poet', but I realise now that he was just trying to get me to take my clothes off.

Now there's an example of how you've changed me, Bessie. Till I met you I hardly ever made jokes about serious events or situations.

Now I do it all the time.

I asked you once why you always made jokes about the grimmest aspects of life and you said "What else can you do about them?"

That stayed with me. Nearly always, the most rational response is a comic one.

Jokes are the last line of defence.

There's another important change that is down to you.

A few months back, I saw a piece about some farmers in India who – in order to scare the monkeys away from their crops – had painted black stripes onto their dogs to try to make them look like tigers.

It's hard to believe any monkeys would fall for that. Tigers move differently, have much bigger builds and tend not to yap.

But what struck me was the photographs of the dogs who had been painted with the tiger-stripes.

To my eyes, they looked self-conscious, almost embarassed. They knew that they made pretty unconvincing tigers. That's what their expressions said to me.

I know how it feels to have some outside agency decide to turn you into an absurd fake.

To the world, it seemed that Zeus had manufactured a superman who was both prodigously strong and totally invulnerable.

Yet, deep down, I knew that I was weak and damaged. That was always a source of great shame for me.

Till now. Thanks to you, it no longer bothers me that I appear to be stronger than I actually am.

"We're *all* acting, Malcolm."
That's one of your catchphrases.
You've made me understand
that.

So now I'm happy to accept
that I'm a painted dog.

And that there is just as
much nobility in a painted
dog as there is in a tiger.

17 minutes.

Right, you need to know that
I have taken one photo as a
memento – the one of you on
that roof watching the swifts.
Also, crucially, you need to
know that although this story
has been populated by an
extraordinary cast of vivid
characters they are *all*
insignificant.

Apart from four. Only four
have a lasting, incalculable,
inextinguishable and
eternal importance to me.
Zeus, I discount.

The only people who genuinely
matter to me are Megara,
our two beautiful children,

who I *didn't* kill, and you.

It was fun, wasn't it, Bessie? You and me. Apart from this last bit.

I've not got the time to read back over what *I've* written so I've no doubt that, structurally, it'll be something of a dog's breakfast and I'm bound to have constantly used two words where one would suffice.

But, for once, I cut loose. To have remained 'a man of few words' – as you often introduced me – would have helped no-one.

Obviously, I have written this account for *you*.

However, if you find it helps, then I won't mind if you choose to show it to other people. Although, they will probably dismiss all these pages as the scribblings of a nutcase. And who could blame them? (Or you)

The times ahead are going to be a wee bit challenging, to put it ~~mildly~~ mildly.

I am so sorry that you'll

have to face a barrage of questions on top of all the anger, shock and loss.

You must do whatever you must to get through it. And if that means hating me, then so be it.

Having lied to you so consistently for so long, I know that I have forfeited the right to retain your love and respect.

It was selfish of me to tie your fate with mine. I hope you find someone who is more deserving and I hope that you won't always curse me for wasting twenty years of your life.

I was often tempted to enter into a deeper commitment, but it would have been irresponsible to start a family when I'm being pursued by a vindictive God. (I know, that old excuse)

If, by some chance, you find

that you don't hate me, then please don't worry about me.

There's no point. Like everyone else, I have no choice but to muddle through.

In the long-term, (very long-term), my future, ultimately, is a mystery that is out of my hands. There may never be a final chapter. It is quite possible, I suppose, that the world will end before I do.

What happens to me if I have no world to inhabit? I have absolutely no idea – which is why it's not worth worrying about.

So don't waste time worrying. And don't waste any time looking for meaning. That's a mug's game. Just enjoy the river-cruise.

OK, I'm cutting it extremely fine now. Just a few more things that I want to tell you for the record.

Everywhere you look, nowadays, you see people striving to be individual with relentless uniformity.

But you'll never do that because you are instinctively original. You don't care what other people think and you know who you are. That's a gift – and it's one of the many things that I'm going to miss, big and small.

Like the renditions of showtunes where the lyrics are ever so slightly incorrect.

And the winter evenings on the sofa when we watched awful movies and played "Guess the Next Line"

And your extraordinary talent for inserting swear-words inside other swear-words.

I'll miss the companionable silences, the faint smell of Olbas oil, the mundane magic of putting out the bins on a Sunday night.

As a young man, I despised the idea of routine. But not here.

Here, I've come to cherish it.

I'm going to hugely miss the sound of your breathing as you lay in the bed alongside me.

Whenever I woke from my nightmares the fact that I could hear you so close always made me feel safe.

I'm going to miss your head cradled against my chest.

The soft brush of your hair. The nape of your neck. The feel of your skin. All the laughter.

That's going to be the biggest absence; the daily intimacy of laughter.

Without that, it's going to be hard to get through the territory.

You're probably dismissing all this as soppy gush. Well, in the nicest possible way, I don't care what you think, my darling, you'll just have to put up with it. Sorry, but I need to say this stuff.

There are many more tributes I would like to embarrass you with, but my taxi driver ~~tross~~

has texted to say he's outside. So this is it, Bessie!

It's cruelly absurd that a man for whom time has no real meaning should be beaten by the clock.

On a practical note, I have transferred most of my savings into your account.

It's just under £2000. I'm sorry it's not more, but it might help tie you over while you get back on your feet.

You're bound to be off work for a fair wee while.

Please don't rush back, Bessie, you're not Superwoman.

That driver's tooting his bloody horn now.

Final thought, my love. Don't dwell on things that can't be changed. Your own words, often.

OK, I'm starting to descend into drivel, so nae more blether.

He's still sounding ~~[illegible]~~ ~~[illegible]~~ his horn! My god, why is everyone so ~~[illegible]~~ impatient!

Well, the man can wait. I'll not be rushed.

Last night I dreamt that I couldn't find my way home. I was driving along the usual route, through all the familiar approach roads, and yet, somehow our house kept drifting further and further away.

It was most frustrating, at first, but then it gradually became terrifying.

When I woke up – in that room at your bedside, – I realized that I'd nodded off for just two or three minutes at the very most.

But I'll not be scared of that dream now, should it return.

Now, deep down, I'm protected by the certainty that in the pin-sharp, film-reel of my memory, in every waking thought, I will always be able to find my way home to you.

As I told you at the start, I forget nothing.

He's tooting again! The world's so bloody noisy today! It's deafening.

I can't think! But it doesn't matter, because there's nothing more to say.

Take care, my darling Bess.

Yours, forever

Malcolm xxxxx

P.S. Apologies I didn't get to fix the boiler. There was a lot going on. Ask Jimmy K to take a look. He's dependable.

P.P.S. The lost city of Atlantis is submerged roughly 35 miles off the south-west tip of Crete. You might be able to monetise this.

P.P.P.S. Just in case you haven't found my keys yet, I didn't want to leave them lying around for anyone to pick up so I've left them under the stone otter.

Life without you is going to be a wee bit drab.

But that's alright, because all that matters is that you are safe now.

OK, my beautiful Bess, that's it. Our time is up.

Unbound is the world's first crowdfunding publisher, established in 2011.

We believe that wonderful things can happen when you clear a path for people who share a passion. That's why we've built a platform that brings together readers and authors to crowdfund books they believe in – and give fresh ideas that don't fit the traditional mould the chance they deserve.

This book is in your hands because readers made it possible. Everyone who pledged their support is listed below. Join them by visiting unbound.com and supporting a book today.

Geoff Adams
John Adams
Keith Adsley
Wyndham Albery
John Allum
Edgar Alves
Douglas Anderson
Graeme Anderson
Judith Anderson
Tom Anderson
Sheila Andrews
Vanessa Andrews
Mark Appleton
Claire Armstrong
Sharon Arthur
Sabrina Artus
Nicola Ashton
Claire Atcheson
Louise Ayling
Vix Ayling
David Baillie
Jason Ballinger
Emily Bamford
Susannah Batstone
Betsy Bearden
Bob Beaupre
Adrian Belcher
David Bell
Paul Bellamy
Calum Benson
Julian Benton
Ray Bewick
John Birtles
Marion Blair
Brenda Blethyn
Philip Blom
Gavin Bluck
Catherine Bolt
Colin Bostock-Smith
Carolyn Braby
Rory Bremner
Tony & Sandie Brent
Joe Broadway
Peter Brooks
Jenny Brophy

Claire Broughton
Chris Brown
Dennis Brown
Margaret JC Brown
Matthew Brown
Damian Browne
David Bryan
Nick and Jane Bryan
Gareth Buchaillard-Davies
Pete Burgess
Ali Burns
Chris Burns
Lazlo Burns
Morris Butler
Matthew Byam Shaw
Michael Cahill
Jo Cameron
Julie Cameron
Grant Campbell
Victoria Cargill-James
Tara Carlisle
Paul Carlyle
Willow Carney
Jonathan Carr
Ben Carter
Stuart Carthy
David Castle
NJ Cesar
Bill & Lindy Chalker
John Charlson
John Charman
Stephen Charman
Paul Child
Erin Christian
Meagan Cihlar
Jenny Clarke
Ian Clarkson
Robert Cole
Maureen Connolly
Chris Cooper
Julian Richard Cooper
Trevor Cooper
Nick Corlett
Rosie Corlett
Andrew Correia
Philip, Beth, Daisy, Max & Sly Cotton
Philipa Coughlan
James Cox
Debbie Crawford
John Crawford
Delwynne Cuttilan
Maarten Leo Daalder
Sarah Dann
Nick Davey
Stuart Davidson
E R Andrew Davis
Hilary Davis
Andrew Dawson
Sean Dawson
David Dent
Veronica Devine
Andy Devonshire
Jenny-Anne Dexter
John Dexter
Max Dighton
Steve Doherty
Marike Dokter
Chris Dottie
Robert Duncan
Celina Dunlop
Robert Eardley
Leah Earl
Barnaby Eaton-Jones
Tanja Eder
Nicky Edmonds
Rob Edwards
Nicholas and Carole Embling
Kenny Endlich
Trish Enright
OMG Hungary Varga Csilla Erika
Herbert Ernst
Lesley Evans
Mike Evens
Martine Farace
Kate Farrell
Rob Farthing
Peter Faulkner
Sarah Felstead
Chris Finnegan
Doug Finnie
Maureen Firth
Colin Fitzpatrick
James Fleet
Alison Fletcher
Daniel Ford
Chris Forster
Mick Freed and Liesel Plikat
Mark French

Neil Gaiman
Tom Galloway
Jill Gamon
Paco B. Garcia
R Gardner
Simon Gardner-Bond
Lisa Gee
Ian Gelsthorpe
Helena Gibbons
Julie Giles
Mark Gillies
Joe Gillis
Jessica Gioia
Laura Glasgow
GMarkC
Oliver Godby
Susan Godfrey
George Goodfellow
Peter A Gordon
Joanne Hackett
Gerry & Anne Hahlo
Steve Hall
Simon Halstead
Isobel Hamilton
Ian Hammond
Alan Hardy
Stephen Harker
Jan Harkin
Pat Harkin
Larry Harper
Simon Harper
Sue Harries
Simon Haslam
Barry Hasler

Martin Hayton
Alan Hazlie
Lindsay Healy
Andrew Hearse
Heather & Thomas
Richard Hein
Robert James Hellyer
Josephine M. Helps
Kate Henriques
Lucy Jane Hess
David Hicks
Stu, Katherine and Izzy Higgins
Mónica Higuera García
Hippy Bamboo Sloth
Peter Michael Hobbins
Jim Hobday
Michael Hodges
Ray Hogan
Mark Hood
Helen Hooker
Jeff Horne
Jon Horne
Antony Howard
Bob Howell
Adam Howie
Howling Dick
Sharon Humphries
Tim & Alison Hunt
Maarit Huotari
John Hutchinson
Nicola Imrie
Yana Ing
Martyn Ingram

Alastair Irons
Stephen Irvin
Ruth Irwin
David Jackson
Judith Jackson
Scott Jackson
Christian Jacobsen
Mike James
Martin and Rosalind Jarvis
Emily Jeffrey
Trevor Jeffrey
Helen Jeffries
Paul Jenkins
Paul Jenner
Phil Jeynes
Alex Jones
Aliy Jones
Andrew Jones
Chris Jones
Claire Jones
Gail Jones
Ian Jones
Liz Jones
Sara Louise Jones
Jack Jordan
Stuart Jordan
Ben Keen
Glenn Kelly
Dan Kieran
Alex King
Deborah King
Will King
Simon Kingston
Warren Lakin

Christopher Lamb
Jonathan Lamb
Gary Lammin
Kerry Lamont
Wendy Lanchin
Roger Langridge
Sara Lednor
David Lees
John Leonard
Sandra Leonard
Imogen Lesser Woods
Claire Lewis
Marian Lewis
Margaret Lewisohn
Robert Lipfriend
Deborah Lloyd
John Lloyd
Charlotte Lo
David Loughlin
Ross Loveland
Eleanor Lowman
David A Luckhurst
Brent Ludwig
Michael Luffingham
Pru Lunberg
Andrew Lunn
Anson Mackay
Helen Maclagan
Karen Macleod
David Manley
Andrew Mann
Nick Manzi
Marlys
Owen Marshall
John & Julie Martin
Kitty Martin
For Martin from Rozie x
Steve Mash
Brian Matson
Tim May
Penny Mayes
Paul Mayhew-Archer
Andrew McAninch
Francis McCabe
John A C McGowan
Gavin McKeown
Kevin McNally
Alec Meadows
Kirsten J. Melbourne
Peter Milburn
Ben Miller
Sarah Milliams
Andrew Mills
Brian Mills
Dianne Mills
Ann Mills-Duggan
Margo Milne
Steven Mitchell
John Mitchinson
Diego Montoyer
Jim Mooney
Alison Morgan
Hayden Morgan
Cara Morris
Jackie Morris
Daniel Morse
George Morton
Ruqayyah Moynihan
Lauren Mulville
Linda Murgatroyd
Barbara Murray
Jon Naismith
Linda Nathan
Carlo Navato
David Neill
Jai Nelson
Simon Newman
Clare Newsome
Roger Noble
Caroline Norris
Alex Norton
Thomas O'Brien
Kate O'Sullivan
Patricia Oakley
James Oddy
Sonia Oldrini
Adrian Oliver
Alex Oliver
Kay Oliver
Simon Oliver
Richard Osman
Dr Alec M Ostler
Justin Owen
Robert Owen
Scott Pack
George Page
Rabindra Paramothayan
Angela Paskins
Jane Passmore
Alex Paterson
Geoff Patterson
Matthew Payne

Nigel Pennington
Anna Perkins
Jeanie & Will Perry
Robert Phillips
Giles Pilbrow
Ralph Plowman
Justin Pollard
Andrew Poole
Lucy Porter
Gill Powell
Lawrence Pretty
Donald Proud
Philip Pullman
Jacqui Pybus
Ben Quant
Brent Quigley
Nicky Quint
Julia Raeburn
Sean Raffey
Duncan Raggett
Robin Rance
Andy Randle
Caroline Raphael
Jeff Rawle
Colette Reap
Debra Reay
Helen Reid
Martin Reithmayr
Nick Revell
Aaron Reynolds
Christine and Neil Richardson
Christopher Richardson
Roly Richardson
Mark Ridgway
Ian Ridley
Liam Riley
Nicola Rimmer
Deb Roberts
Tony Roberts
Wyn Roberts
Dan & Kate Robinson
Stian Rødland
Colin Rogers
Lorraine Rogerson
David Rose
Chana Rochel Ross
Julie Round
Catherine Rowlands
Oliver Rowley
Alistair Rush
Kevin Ryder
Madeline Ryder
Ruth-Anne Sahin
Deepali Sanganee
Neil Saunders
Tony Sawford
Saskia Schuster
Matthew Scott
Jason Searle
Melanie Sharpe
Andrew Shead
David Shelley
Danielle Sherman
Jodi Shields
Andrew Shone
David Shriver
Mel Shuttleworth
Alan Sims
Pete Sinclair
Katie Skidmore
Sara-Jayne Slack
Keith Sleight
Rosie Smeaton
Andrew Smith
Michael Soares
Kerri J Spangaro
Amanda Sparks
Rachel Speed
Rita Spencer
Conor Stainton-Polland
Vicki Stannard
Ros Stern
Patrick Stevens
Paul Stevens
Rachel Stockdale
Bill Stone
Roger Stone
Mair Stratton
Ken Stringer
Alistair Struth
Nina Tawton-Hughes
Alan D Taylor
Georgette Taylor
Richard Taylor
Andrew Tees
Will Templeton
Eileen Thomas
Richard Thomas
David Thompson
Jemma Thompson
Sue Thompson

James Thorpe
Roger Thorpe
Matthew Tiller
Lydia Timpson
Dawn Toland
Neil Tomlinson
Lucy Traves
Christopher Tredway
Stephen Trotman
Martin Trotter
David Turnbull
Mark Turner
Mike Turner
Mark Vent
Richard Visick
Nick Wadlow
Julia Wagner Grover
Ian Walker
Steve Walker
Dj Walker-Morgan
Katie Wallbanks
Lynne Wallbanks
Ulf Wallentin
Nick Walpole
Joseph Walsh
Keith Walton
Ian Warburton
Eli Ward
James P Ward
Lynda Waterhouse
Andrew Weaver
Christoph Weis
Pam Whetnall
Richard Whitaker
Albert W I White
James White
Sue Whitehead
Darren Whitworth
Vicky Wicks
Dave Williams
Neil Williams
Nick Williams
Ross Williams
Sean Williams
Catherine Williamson
Aaron Wilson
Derek Wilson
Susan Wilson
Martin Winch
Stephen Wise
Johanna Wolf
Peter Wood
James Woods
Jim Woods
Kim Woods
Wendalynn Wordsmith
Sharon Wright
Debbie Wythe
Simon Yates
Terri Young